Also by Michelle Gordon:

*Earth Angel Series:*

The Earth Angel Training Academy

The Earth Angel Awakening

The Other Side

The Twin Flame Reunion

*Visionary Collection:*

Heaven dot com

The Doorway to PAM

The Elphite

I'm Here

*Oracle Cards:*

Aria's Oracle

Velvet's Oracle

Amethyst's Oracle

# The Twin Flame Retreat

Michelle Gordon

theamethystangel.com

All rights reserved; no part of this book may be reproduced, stored in a retrieval system, or transmitted, in any form or by any means, without the prior permission in writing from the publisher, nor be otherwise circulated in any form of binding or cover other than that in which it is published and without a similar condition including this condition being imposed on the subsequent purchaser.

First published in Great Britain in 2015 by The Amethyst Angel

Copyright © 2015 by Michelle Gordon

Cover illustration by madappledesigns

Copyright © The Amethyst Angel

ISBN: 978-1508605171

The moral right of the author has been asserted.

All characters and events in this publication, other than those clearly in the public domain are fictitious, and any resemblance to real persons, living or dead, is purely coincidental.

First Edition

# Gratitude

I feel so utterly blessed to have been helped by so many people to bring my books to print and get them out into the world.

The following people all know how they have helped, and I want to express my gratitude to them for all they've done:
Mum, Jon, Liz Gordon, Chip, Megan Hiscox, Anne, Kelly, Niki and Dan, Lucja Fratczak-Kay, Sarah Vine, Loubie Lou, Hannah Imogen Jones, Angela Raasch, Miranda Adams, Tiffany Hathorn, Janina Irvin, Dawn, Willow, Helen Gordon, Richard Grey, Annette Ecuyere, Rosa Lewis, Wenna Macormac, Cyndi Sabido, Janet Spillane Gupwell, Robyn Peters, Emerald, Xander, Andrew Embling, Valerie Abl and Alexandra Payne.

I would like to share a letter of gratitude to Elizabeth Lockwood, my friend for the last 23 years. You can also watch the video I made for Liz on my gratitude page - twinflameblog.com/gratitude.

Dear Liz,

I want to thank you with my whole heart, you have not just been a friend to me for the last 23 years, you have been my supporter, my editor, my proof-reader, and you have shone your light in very dark times. You were there whenever I needed someone to talk to, and I can only hope that I have returned the love and support when you have needed it.

You inspire me every day with your drive and determination; how you have managed to run so many marathons, I have no idea. I often wish that I had even an ounce of your motivation! You have raised so much money for amazing charities, all while experiencing some of the darkest times of your life.

More than anyone else I know, you deserve a beautiful life, filled with Angels, love and rainbows! I feel incredibly lucky to be able to call you my friend, and I hope you will accept 50% ownership of this book as a dedication of my love and gratitude to you.

I love you Angel,
Michelle
xxx

This book is dedicated to my beautiful Angel friend,
Elizabeth Lockwood.

# Chapter One

A whole year had passed since Aria had left, and yet his home still felt empty without her giggling presence. Tim stared at the computer screen and sighed. He had immersed himself in his work, in growing his business, in the hope it would fill the hole left behind by the crazy Faerie.

His gaze was caught by a postcard pinned on his noticeboard. Aria had sent it to him from India, where she was travelling with Linen. He was happy that she was so happy, after all, unhappy Faeries were not a good thing. But he couldn't help but wish it were him she was with, not Linen.

He sighed again and refocused his attention on the screen. An email popped up from an address he was unfamiliar with. He was just about to put it in the Junk folder when the subject headline caught his attention.

Looking for your Twin Flame?

Frowning, he clicked on it. Apart from when Aria had been there, he had never come across the term 'Twin Flame' and knowing how sure Aria was that Linen was hers, he was intrigued to know more. The email opened and he read through it quickly. It was an ad for a course at the Twin Flame Retreat, which offered meditations, workshops and healing, centred around bringing Twin Flames together. Out of curiosity, he clicked on the link, and visited the website. His eyes widened when he saw the picture of the couple called Violet and Greg who ran the retreat. He was sure that the woman was Velvet.

A younger version perhaps, but it certainly looked like the woman he had memories of.

He wondered how they had managed to get his email address. He couldn't remember signing up to a mailing list. He knew that Aria would say it was a sign from the Angels. And perhaps it was. Without thinking too much about it, Tim clicked on the booking page, and filled in his details, booking the next available weekend session. He really needed to move on from Aria, to let her go and find the one that he was supposed to be with. She must be out there somewhere, Tim thought to himself as he filled in his credit card details and paid for the weekend. It seemed like Violet had also written a book, called The Earth Angel Training Academy, which was available to buy. Again, with little thought, he ordered the book and he decided he needed a break from the screen. So he put his computer into hibernation mode, got up, slipped on his jacket, shoved his feet into his shoes then left his flat.

He found himself walking to the park without even thinking about it, and he stood on the spot where he had met Aria. Why couldn't he let her go?

Perhaps it was because he had felt such a connection to her. No doubt because they had spent time in another dimension together. Being with her had felt so easy and natural, which wasn't normal for him. He often found it difficult to relate to others, and Aria had teased him it was because he was an alien. He smiled, and realised that he missed her teasing, her jokes and the silliness. He felt like he hadn't had fun since she'd left. His shoulders slumped and he stared down at the ground. He felt pathetic.

"Hey, Alien."

His head whipped round, and as though he had conjured her up from his thoughts, Aria stood before him. A grin lit up her face and she threw her arms around him.

"Aria!" he gasped, as he hugged her back tightly. "Where did you come from? I thought you were still in India with Linen?"

- 2 -

Aria pulled and smiled. "We got back a few days ago. It was amazing! You really should go some day. I came to see you, and you weren't in, so I thought I'd walk home the scenic way. I'm glad I found you though."

"I'm glad you did too," Tim said softly, studying her face intently. "I've missed you."

Aria sighed. "I missed you too, Tim. Did you get my postcards?"

"Yes, I did. Do you want to come back for a cup of tea?"

"Yes, I would like that a lot."

Tim held out his arm. Aria took it, and they walked arm in arm back to his flat. Tim's heart was singing as she chattered away about her adventures.

When they got back to his place, he made them both tea, then they sat on the sofa and she continued chattering away. If he was truthful, Tim wasn't really listening, though he was making the appropriate noises in the right places. He was just enjoying the feeling of her company again.

"So how is the Zoo going? I do miss working there, it was a lot of fun."

Tim snapped to attention at the direct question and blinked. "It's doing well, I've taken on new staff who are working well, though I have yet to find anyone who has as much knowledge of and affinity with the butterflies as you did. I've even taken on a manager so I don't have to be there every day."

"That's great! Of course you need to just find a few more Faeries to work with the butterflies. Though as you know, they're not always very reliable."

Tim chuckled. "True. They are a lot of fun though. So things are good with you and Linen?"

Aria frowned a little at his tone, but nodded. "Yes, we've had our ups and downs, but then we were like that in the Fifth Dimension too. Linen has had to be really organised in order to make our travels work, and I know he finds that difficult, after all, he is a Faerie. But then he had plenty of practice as the assistant head at the Academy. It's just not something that comes naturally. And we feel we have been fulfilling our missions to Awaken everyone we meet. I think we will probably travel more in the coming years. I don't think either of us is keen to settle down." She grinned, and Tim's heart melted. "We're Faeries, we need to fly."

Tim sighed. "Yes, you do." He set his empty cup down. "You know if you need any work, in-between your travels, that your place at the Zoo is always there for you."

Aria giggled. "That makes me sound like some kind of jungle animal."

Tim laughed. "Yes it did, I'm sorry, that's not what I meant at all."

Aria patted his arm, and his skin tingled from her touch. "I know, I was just teasing."

There were a few moments of silence then, and Tim couldn't help but gaze into Aria's eyes. After a few seconds, she blinked and looked away, a look of confusion on her face. She slurped down the rest of her tea, then set her cup down on the coffee table too.

"I should go. Linen will be expecting me home."

Tim nodded, but his heart was protesting. "Of course, I could walk you home, or call you a cab?"

"Don't be silly, I'll be fine. But thank you." Aria stood up to leave and Tim followed suit. They went to the door, and Aria gathered up her coat and shoes on the way. At the front door, she stopped and turned to him. "It was good to see you Tim, I'm glad you're okay."

"I'm glad you're okay too, Aria."

She leaned over and kissed him on the cheek, then opened the door. Just as she stepped through, she looked over her shoulder. "Goodbye, Alien."

"Goodbye, Faerie," Tim replied. When the door closed behind her, he stood there for a long time. It felt so surreal. Just hours before, he had been wishing he could see her, and she had just appeared out of nowhere. But despite his feelings

- 4 -

for her, one thing was clear - she was Linen's Flame, not his. And he needed to let go.

Before he could stop himself, he went around his small flat, removing all traces of Aria. Postcards, photos of them both, little notes she had written, he put them all into a shoebox, and then tucked it away at the bottom of his wardrobe.

Once he had done that, he went to the fridge and pulled out a beer, then sat in front of the TV, and watched whatever was on the first channel he came to. As he watched the images on the screen, he barely noticed the tears trickling down his cheeks.

\*      \*      \*

The journey had been such a long one. But finally, Amy was pulling her trusty campervan into the tiny, bumpy lane that led to the Twin Flame Retreat. She had been away for six months, travelling around Europe with Fay, and they had just got back from France a few days before. Even though she felt exhausted, she couldn't wait to go and visit Violet and Greg, it felt like she hadn't seen them for ages.

She winced a little as the rocky track scraped the underneath of her van, and was relieved a few minutes later to pull into the parking space. She stared at the wooden sign of the retreat, and smiled as she remembered the first time she and Violet had stayed there. They'd had no idea, at that point, of what the next few years were to hold for them both. Though she had yet to meet her own Flame, Amy was so pleased that Violet had found hers.

She jumped out of the van and opened the side door to grab her case, then she slammed the door shut and locked it, though out here, who would bother stealing it? She dragged her case up the path toward the house, and a feeling of being home stole over her. She really loved being in the middle of the woods.

She reached the front door and rang the bell, and a few seconds later, the door opened and Violet stood there, a huge smile on her face.

"Angel! You're home!"

Amy laughed and threw her arms around the Old Soul. "I am indeed." They hugged for a while, then Violet grabbed her case and ushered her inside. Amy looked around the front room, pleased to see that though it looked much the way it had when Esmeralda and Mike had been there, it had a few touches of Violet and Greg now too.

"It's so weird to be back here," Amy said, as her gaze caught sight of the photo of the two Angels.

Violet followed her gaze and sighed. "I know what you mean. Sometime, upon waking in the morning, I forget that they have left us. I think their energy has remained here in some way."

"I'm so glad they left this place to you guys. That the retreats will continue. People need them if they are going to reunite with their Flames."

"It's funny," Violet said, as they went through into the kitchen. "We have had to start offering a different kind of Twin Flame Retreat recently, for those who have met their Flames, but aren't with them for whatever reason."

Amy raised her eyebrows and removed her coat. "Well I can't think of anyone better suited to help someone through that than you."

Violet smiled, but looked a bit embarrassed. She turned and busied herself with making them tea. "I guess. It just breaks my heart having to comfort poor souls who are apart from their Flames. It really isn't something I would wish for anyone to have to experience."

"I know, but at least by meeting and working with you, they will see that it is in fact possible to survive it. And that it's important that they do. Their missions on this planet are so important."

"Yes, they are. Speaking of which, I want to hear all about

- 6 -

your adventures across Europe with Fay." Violet poured their drinks and they went into the lounge and made themselves comfortable on the settee.

"Where to begin? We spent a lot of time in Italy, the scenery there is just so breath-taking it made me want to become an artist, or a photographer. But then even that wouldn't capture how it felt to be there. The energy is so different, you really should visit one day."

Violet sighed. "I would love to, but I'm not sure that will happen right now."

Amy frowned and looked more closely at her friend. Despite her makeup, she could see dark circles under her eyes, and a tiredness in her expression. "How are things with you and Greg?"

Violet smiled, knowing that Amy had sensed something. "It's not been the easiest year, I will admit. After Esmeralda and Mike passed away, there was a lot of legal stuff that had to be sorted, and we were met with a lot of resistance from their families, who hated the fact that they had left the retreat to us and not them. So it was a bit of a battle, and at times, we nearly gave up, and just handed it over to them. The only thing that stopped us was knowing that Esmeralda and Mike would have hated that." Violet took a sip of her drink, and Amy nodded for her to continue.

"Once that was all settled, we then had to learn how to run the place. I mean, we had done it a little while we were here with Mike, but all we'd done was run the workshops. We hadn't done any of the paperwork, and the business side of things. And to be honest when we actually went through the financial stuff, we started to wonder what we had let ourselves in for." Violet shook her head. "It seems that running a Twin Flame Retreat isn't the most lucrative business in the world. Which is why I have been doing some part-time work locally, and why Greg has been odd jobbing around the area too."

Amy's eyes widened. "I had no idea, I thought it was doing really well."

"I guess it didn't help that we had to cancel all the retreats for a few months. It's taken a while to rebuild the reputation of the centre. We did contact everyone who had their bookings cancelled and we explained the situation. Most of them were very understanding, but some were less so."

"I'm so sorry it's been so difficult for you." Amy frowned. "I hope it hasn't affected you both too much?"

Tears welled up in Violet's eyes. "It hasn't had a positive effect. Greg and I have talked a few times about breaking up."

Amy shook her head. "No, seriously? That's crazy. It would be better to sell this place and leave together than for one of you to leave the other here, surely?"

Violet shrugged. "I don't know. Greg has really settled down here, I don't think he wants to leave. But the financial situation is a bit of a strain, and I don't know, part of me doesn't feel like it's my mission to remain in one place. I feel like I need to be free to move around more. I also want to promote my book."

"Of course! Have you got a copy here? I wanted to get one as soon as it was out, but I didn't have an address I could use while we were travelling to get it sent to me."

"You could have got the eBook version," Violet teased. She stood up and went over to the bookshelf. She pulled a book down and then handed it to Amy.

Amy smiled when she saw the cover. "Oh, Violet, it's beautiful! You must be so pleased. I can't wait to read it."

"You can keep that copy. I have more. I could sign it for you, but I doubt that will make it worth millions."

Amy giggled. "You never know, one day it might." She flicked through the pages, feeling proud of her friend for writing about the Earth Angels.

"How did you publish it in the end?"

"I did it myself. I looked at all the options, and quite honestly, I didn't like the idea of traditional publishing. It could have taken months, maybe years, to even just find an agent. And then you have no control over the process. So I did it all independently. But of course, that wasn't particularly cheap to do. I was lucky to find an incredible editor, and a great graphics guy, who designed the covers. But it was a fairly crazy process. I had no idea there was so much to do, when you do it all yourself. I'm not sure I would do it all again."

"There's no sequel?" Amy asked.

Violet laughed. "Who knows? Maybe there will be. But for now, I would like to just sell enough copies of this one to make back the money I spent on publishing it. Quite a few of the retreat participants have been buying copies, which is great, and I have a few really good reviews so far. But if I thought the publishing process was complex, the whole marketing thing, well, don't get me started."

"How much is it? I would like to purchase this one."

Violet waved her hand. "Oh don't be silly. You can have that one, you're my closest friend."

"I'm not being silly. As your closest friend, I want to support you in any way I can." Amy dug around in her handbag for her purse and pulled out a ten pound note. She handed it to Violet. "Will that cover it?"

Violet hesitated before taking it. Then finally she smiled and accepted it. "Thank you, yes, it will. I do appreciate it, Angel."

"I know you do." Amy yawned then, suddenly overcome with tiredness.

"I'll show you to the guest room. Greg and I have finally moved into the main room. It felt too weird at first, knowing that's where Esmeralda passed away. But actually, we've found that it makes us feel closer to them somehow."

Amy stood up and Violet followed suit. Amy put her arms around the Old Soul and hugged her tight. "I am sure they are watching over you two, and that they are sending all their love and light your way."

"I hope so."

*　　*　　*

"Oh my goodness! She's growing so fast!"

Starlight smiled at her friend, who was holding her daughter, Star. "That she is," she agreed. "I can't believe she will be a year old in a couple of months. It's just flown by."

Hannah nodded. "It is going by so fast. And yet, I feel myself beginning to get impatient." She looked down at Star's sleeping face, and bit her lip. "I feel so ready to meet my Flame, or at least a soulmate with whom I can share my life and my mission with."

Starlight nodded. "I can imagine that it was quite frustrating to see me enter Earth and almost immediately meet my soulmate and begin a family."

Hannah laughed. "I am so happy for you, you know that. But yes, it was a little frustrating. It feels like I have been looking for so long."

"Maybe you haven't been looking in the right places."

"Maybe," Hannah agreed with a sigh. She tilted her head to one side. "Is Gareth your Twin Flame?"

Starlight looked toward the door, as though checking to make sure he was out of earshot. Hannah could hear the TV playing in the living room where he was watching a rugby game. Starlight looked back to her and shook her head.

"No, Gareth is not my Twin Flame. Though I do believe he is an Earth Angel, because he's so supportive of me and what I am here to do."

"Aren't you afraid that if you're with Gareth you will miss out on meeting your Twin Flame? I mean, what if he's out there, waiting for you, and you're here with Gareth?"

"You're right about one thing, he is out there, and he is waiting for me, but I won't miss out on meeting him because he is not on this planet at this time. He has remained on the Other Side."

Hannah's eyes widened. "Oh, I'm sorry. I didn't realise." Suddenly, she felt a tug of connection through her Indigo

- 10 -

awareness, and she found herself looking up at a tall man with grey hair and golden robes. She blinked and gasped. "Gold? He is your Flame?"

It was Starlight's turn to look shocked. "How did you know that?"

"I just saw him, through one of my siblings, who seems to be with him at this time, for some reason. It was too fleeting a connection to determine the reason. Wow, Gold is your Flame. That is really quite incredible. But then, considering who you are that makes perfect sense."

"Yes, I guess it does. But we have not had a lifetime together for a very long time. Once my mission is complete here, I will return to the stars, and he will return with me. My guess is, that your sibling is there to learn how to take over from him."

Hannah didn't know what to say. Her mind was whirring. "An Indigo Child is taking Gold's place?"

"I would assume so, that would have been my recommendation. After all, the wisdom of the Indigos goes beyond what we Old Souls can comprehend. Who better to advise the souls who are crossing back to the Other Side?"

Hannah gazed into baby Star's eyes as she awoke in her arms. Star stared back at her, her bright blue eyes taking in everything. "Hey," Hannah whispered. "You have a very beautiful and amazing Mummy, did you know that?"

As if she understood every word, Star smiled and looked over at Starlight, who smiled back.

"She's a crystal child?" Hannah asked.

Starlight nodded. "Yes she is. I can sense her crystal energy. It reminds me of being on the crystal planet."

"That's amazing. Was it much like ours?"

Starlight shook her head. "No, it was much like Earth, only with endless fields of flowers and caves full of crystals. It was quite stunning."

"What about the Rainbow planet? What was that like?"

Starlight shook her head. "That was even more breath-

- 11 -

taking, it had -"

"Sarah, honey?"

Starlight stopped mid-sentence and looked up at Gareth who was stood in the doorway. "Yes, Sweetie?"

"When are we having dinner?"

Hannah looked down at Star to hide her smile. Compared to the conversation the two women were enjoying, having someone to interrupt to ask about dinner was really incongruous.

"I will start it in a minute. I was planning on making pizza."

Gareth nodded. "Okay, cool, so in about an hour then?"

"Yes, about an hour," Starlight agreed. Gareth went back into the living room, and Starlight grinned at Hannah. "Oh the joys of human needs eh?"

Hannah giggled. "I was just thinking how incredibly mundane it seemed, compared to what we were talking about."

Starlight got up and started pulling ingredients out of the fridge and cupboards while Star and Hannah watched. "Would you like to stay for dinner with us?"

Hannah thought about her empty flat, with no one waiting for her and nothing but a mouldy bit of cheese in the fridge for dinner and she nodded enthusiastically. "Yes, please."

"Excellent. It's only frozen pizza with added toppings and some frozen potato wedges though I'm afraid. I haven't quite figured out this cooking lark, to be honest with you."

Hannah chuckled. "Don't worry, I have been on Earth for twenty-five years now, and even I have trouble with the cooking lark."

Starlight laughed and started chopping up a red pepper then grated some cheese. Hannah contented herself with making faces at Star, who stared up at her in amusement.

Forty-five minutes later, they all sat around the table, and chatted about general things. Gareth wasn't in much of a mood to chat as his team had lost the game.

"So how is work going?" Starlight asked Hannah, for lack

- 12 -

of anything else normal to talk about.

Hannah smiled. "It's okay, nothing interesting has happened recently. I'm thinking of a career change, actually. I used to feel like I needed to be in that job, but I really haven't felt that way for a few months now." She shared a smile with Starlight, who knew that the reason was likely to be because she needed to be there to assist Starlight when she got to Earth.

"What are you thinking of doing instead?"

Hannah sighed. "Well that's the thing. I have no idea. I would need to retrain for something else. And possibly move somewhere smaller if it doesn't pay as much."

Starlight was quiet for a while, and Hannah wondered if she was connecting with the divine again. It amazed and awed her at how easily she connected with divine wisdom. Hannah vowed silently to meditate more, she needed to feel more connected.

"I think you should check your email," Starlight said.

Hannah's frowned. "Umm, okay, I'll check it when I get back."

"Excellent."

The rest of the meal passed in silence, and Hannah suddenly felt impatient so that she could get home and check her email. She could have checked it on her phone, but she had deliberately left it at home so she could concentrate on just being with her friend and not get distracted. She got home just after ten o'clock, and ran up the stairs to her apartment. She went inside and went straight to her phone which was faster than her laptop. She clicked on her email and scrolled through. Just as Starlight had predicted there was a very interesting email in her inbox, from the Twin Flame Retreat with the subject heading – Are you looking for your Twin Flame?

She opened it and scanned it quickly, and within seconds, she knew that she had found what she needed. She went over to her laptop, and before she had even taken off her coat and shoes, she went online and booked her place on the next Twin Flame retreat.

- 14 -

# Chapter Two

"Yes, I know he's your favourite character, but there's just something not quite, right about him," Beatrice said, trying to be tactful. "I just don't think the reader will relate to him, and then they'll give up on the story. He needs to have at least one redeeming feature." Beatrice listened to her author defend her creation for ten minutes before silently admitting defeat. "Okay, we'll look at him again later, shall we move onto the next point?"

After an hour, Beatrice hung up the phone, feeling like she'd been through a terrible ordeal. She got up from her desk and went to the kitchen to make herself a cup of tea.

"Authors," she muttered to her cat, Harry. "Think they know it all! Think they don't need any editing, or any help! Happy to put out any old rubbish." She sloshed the hot water onto her instant coffee and then added milk, stirring it a bit too vigorously. "And then when the bad reviews come rolling in, somehow it will all be my fault!"

She returned to her desk in her tiny home office with the coffee and a packet of biscuits, sat down, and smiled as Harry immediately took his place across her feet. Despite her workload, she decided to procrastinate a little by checking her email. She saw one from Violet, one of her authors, and opened it. It was a reminder to book her place on an upcoming Twin Flame retreat. Though she had enjoyed editing Violet's book, she wasn't sure she really believed in all the spiritual stuff it covered. And Twin Flames? Really? The idea of there being one person out there who was perfect for you, just seemed a bit too farfetched. But then what did she have to lose by attending? The retreat was a gift from Violet to her, it would be rude not to go. She opened up the booking page and booked her place, entering the special code Violet had sent her. Then she closed her emails and returned to her current editing project. It was not the most thrilling text in the world, and despite her passion for grammar and punctuation, it was a bit of an arduous task.

Two hours later, her alarm went off and she cheered. She had been looking forward to that evening for a couple of weeks. It was her friend's birthday and they were checking out a new restaurant in town that had recently opened. Working from home made Beatrice appreciate social events much more, and she found that if she went more than three days just talking to Harry or to her clients, then she started to go a little bit crazy.

After backing up her files and shutting down her computer, Beatrice headed for the shower, before figuring out what to wear. It wasn't a fancy restaurant, but she wanted to look nice for the occasion. It took twenty minutes to decide, but finally, she emerged from her bedroom, dressed and ready to go. She fed Harry, who purred in appreciation.

"Do you think I made the right choice?" she asked him. She did a little twirl, but he was too busy eating his food to notice. She sighed. "I can't believe I'm asking my cat if I look okay." Shaking her head, she left her house, and headed down the street to the bus stop. Ordinarily, she would have driven into town, but tonight she wanted to be able to have a few glasses of wine with her girlfriends. After what seemed like an age, she boarded the bus into town, and nabbed a seat near the back. She had purposely left her phone behind, not wanting to be distracted by work, but was regretting the decision, as she had nothing to occupy her time while the bus ambled into town.

She stared out of the window, her mind still half on her current project, and half on the Twin Flame retreat. She had no idea what to expect; Violet had assured her it would just be some meditations and workshops, but what did that mean? She had never been the kind of person to meditate. Clear your mind? Yeah, sure. Editors didn't have clear minds; they had plots and characters and red herrings all yelling for attention. She hadn't even met Violet in person. They had only spoken on the phone and through email. Though it had seemed like the right thing to do, Beatrice was beginning to regret booking the retreat already.

When the bus pulled up in the town centre, Beatrice got off, and made her way to the restaurant. She was a little later than planned, but she was sure she wouldn't have missed much. She headed toward the table shrouded in balloons and as soon as Chloe saw her she squealed in delight and ran over to her, engulfing her in a hug. Beatrice laughed.

"Happy birthday!" She gave Chloe her gift, wrapped up in her favourite colour, and Chloe immediately ripped it open, squealing again when she saw what was inside.

"Thank you! I've been wanting to read this for ages!"

"It's a signed copy too," Beatrice said, pulling out a chair at the table and sitting down with the rest of the party.

"That's amazing! How did you pull that one off?"

"Ah ha," Beatrice said, tapping her nose. "I have a few connections."

Chloe grinned and hugged the book to her chest. "That's awesome. How are things going with the editing?"

Beatrice waved her hand dismissively. "Let's not talk work, it's your birthday. I'm sure someone else must have something much more interesting to share."

"Well, Ewan and I weren't going to tell anyone yet, but I can't wait any longer," Jade said. "I'm pregnant!"

"Oh my goodness!" Chloe screamed, throwing her arms around her friend. Everyone started congratulating the couple and asking what the sex was, and when she was due, but

Beatrice couldn't bring herself to join in. She sipped her water and wished she hadn't said anything.

Would it ever stop hurting? She was sure that her inability to have children was what had stopped her from seeking out 'the one'. Why would anyone want to marry her when they would be unable to have a family? No, it was better just to be happy with Harry. He understood her. Her mind wandered to the upcoming retreat again. What was the point of going? She didn't believe that her Twin Flame existed. And if he did, why would he want to be with her?

Having survived several hours of baby-talk (only by downing several glasses of wine) Beatrice managed to get herself home, and stumbled through the door of her house. She slammed the door behind her, not caring that it was one in the morning, and went straight to the kitchen to get some water. She knew she would regret her drinking binge during her workout in the morning, but maybe if she drank enough water now, she could limit the fuzziness.

She drank until her bladder was fit to burst, then got herself ready for bed. She smiled when she saw Harry curled up on her bed, but then without warning, she started to sob. Harry woke up at the sound and peered at her in concern, which made her cry harder. She pulled the covers back, got in beside him, and cried herself to sleep, while stroking his soft black fur, and feeling his purr vibrating thorough her hand.

\*　　\*　　\*

Mary moved to the music, completely oblivious to the people around her, all of whom were slick with sweat like her. The beat of the music throbbed in her chest, and eyes closed, she revelled in the almost out-of-body experience. Considering the amount of alcohol she had consumed earlier in the evening, it was amazing she was even able to remain upright, but somehow, she kept on dancing.

"Here, try this."

She opened her eyes and found a small white pill being offered to her by a very cute guy. With a shrug, she accepted the pill and swallowed it dry. Then she closed her eyes again and kept dancing. She was vaguely aware of the body pressed up close to hers, but it didn't bother her. She knew she could handle herself.

"Do you want to get out of here?" the voice asked. She nodded in reply, and felt him take her hand. She allowed herself to be led out of the club, and when they left the warmth and were hit by a blast of cool air, her eyes popped open and her last shred of common sense resurfaced. She stopped suddenly and pulled her hand free of his. She squinted at him, but found that her sight was a little blurry.

"What is it, baby? Let's go back to mine."

She shook her head, and he leaned closer so that the bouncer who stood nearby, watching them, wouldn't overhear. "Come with me now, I promise you will have an amazing time."

"Hey, Miss, are you okay?"

Mary looked up at the bouncer and shook her head, she tried to speak, but nothing would come out. She couldn't seem to get her brain to function properly. But the bouncer had clearly seen enough. "Can I call someone for you?" he asked, moving in-between her and the guy.

"Hey, buddy, it's cool, I'm taking her home now, she's just had a few too many that's all, I'll make sure she's okay."

The bouncer frowned, and Mary was afraid he would believe him. He turned to her again. "Miss, do you even know this guy?"

She shook her head again, and with that movement, found herself falling forward. The bouncer must have caught her, because the impact was a soft one just as she blacked out.

"Mary? Mary can you hear me?"

Her eyelids felt like they weighed a ton each, as Mary tried to open her eyes. When she finally managed it, she regretted it instantly. Everything was far too white.

"Oh, shit," she muttered. "Am I dead?"

"As hard as you tried, I'm afraid you're still alive," the slightly sarcastic voice replied. "You're in hospital. In A&E. The nightclub called an ambulance when they couldn't wake you up. You're lucky they did, your temperature was dangerously high."

Eyes still closed, Mary nodded in response. Despite feeling relieved she was still alive, a tiny part of her was upset. Surely the Other Side had to be better than here?

"Is there anyone we can contact? We will need to discharge you into someone's care."

Mary pulled a face. "My dad, I guess. Can you wait until a bit later though? I don't think I can face him right now."

"Okay, I will get his number from you in a while. Just try to rest, we have you on an IV to get some fluids into you, you were also extremely dehydrated. There's some water on your bedside table, try to drink as much as you can too."

Mary nodded, but as soon as she heard the footsteps moving away, she slipped into a blissful unconsciousness again.

"Mary! Are you okay?!"

Without even opening her eyes, Mary recognised her sister's soft voice and she groaned inwardly. Knowing that she wouldn't give up easily, she pried an eye open and saw her sister stood there, her hands on her hips, and the concern on her face marred slightly by the disapproval and disappointment in her eyes.

"Hey, Sis. I know, I know, I'm in a state again."

"They said that the bouncer stopped a guy from taking you home with him! Did you have any concept at all of the danger you put yourself in? He could have raped and murdered you! I really don't want to get that call from the police, being called by the hospital was bad enough. Dad was so upset I insisted I would come and get you instead." She came closer to the bed, and put her hand on Mary's arm when she saw the tears welling up in her eyes.

"What are we going to do with you, Mare? I know I tell you off, but it's only because I don't know what I would do if I lost you."

The tears spilled down Mary's cheeks, and she regretted all of the pain she had caused her family over the years. But since her mother had died, she just couldn't get herself together.

"I know you miss Mum, I do too. But this has gone on for too long now."

Mary nodded, and her sister leant forward to hug her, careful not to pull on the tubes attached to Mary's arms.

"I'll go see when you're allowed out, you're coming home with me, okay?"

Mary nodded and watched her sister leave the cubicle, grateful that she hadn't lectured her too much. A couple of hours later, she was deemed fit to discharge, and she let her sister lead her out to her car, and help her get in like she was a child.

"Are you hungry?" she asked.

Mary's stomach grumbled in response and they both laughed.

"I'll take that as a yes." Her sister pulled out onto the main road and was quiet while she concentrated on navigating the traffic.

Now sober, and clear headed, Mary felt her anxieties and fears creeping back in, and she sighed. Her sister noticed the sound.

"What is it?" she asked.

"I'm so sorry, for putting you through this, Celine, I really don't mean to be such a pain in the backside all the time. But," Mary took a deep breath. She had never admitted this to anyone. "I just find it really hard to be here sometimes. To be human." She tried to laugh. "I know that probably sounds ridiculous, and I wouldn't blame you for turning round and taking me straight back to the psych ward, but it's how I feel. I drink and I take stuff, because I don't know how to be here."

Tears spilled down her cheeks and Celine was quiet for a few moments.

"You may not believe me, but I actually do know what you mean, and how you feel. Because I often feel the same way."

Eyes wide, Mary turned to look at her sister. "Really? But you always have everything together. You have your work and your house and you seem to be so happy."

Celine smiled. "I'm very thankful for all the blessings I have in my life, but as perfect as it all may seem, sometimes I feel so lonely, so desperate to go home, that it's unbearable."

Mary didn't respond for a while. She couldn't believe that her perfect sister felt the same. "Why do we feel this way?"

Celine sighed. "If I tell you what I think, I fear you may think I'm crazy."

Mary laughed. "It can't be that far out, surely?"

"Tell you what, rather than me trying to explain it, I'll lend you a book that will explain it all."

Mary groaned. "A book? Can't you just give me the summary? You know I hate reading."

"It's a novel, a story. And it's very readable. Honestly, while you're in bed recovering, it wouldn't hurt to give it a go."

"I guess." The rest of the short journey passed in silence, and when they reached Celine's house, Mary was feeling ravenous.

She helped herself to a bowl of cereal while Celine boiled some eggs and made some toast. Mary gulped down her breakfast while Celine watched her and drank her coffee. She disappeared for a few minutes and then came back with a book and set it in front of Mary.

Mary brushed the crumbs off her fingers onto her leggings and picked it up, silently reading the title. "Are you sure you can't just tell me what it's about?"

Celine shook her head. "Read it. Then we'll talk again about not feeling like we belong here." She got up from the

- 22 -

table and cleared away some of the dishes. "I have to get to work now, I'm on the afternoon shift. Will you be okay?"

Mary nodded, feeling bad to have taken up her sister's free morning; she knew she worked really hard as a care assistant in an old people's home. "I'll be fine. Thank you, for coming to get me. I appreciate it."

"You're welcome. Enjoy the book."

By the time Celine left a few minutes later, Mary had already started reading the novel. She found herself completely absorbed in the story. Her ass went numb, sitting at the dining table, so she made herself another cup of tea and moved to the sofa, and she was still there, eight hours later, when Celine returned.

"Well, I can't say I'm surprised," Celine said as she joined Mary on the sofa. "I knew you'd get into it."

"I haven't moved all day!" Mary said.

"I can see that," Celine commented. She got up and went to the kitchen to start making dinner, and Mary followed, groaning a little as she straightened her stiff limbs.

"Do Velvet and Laguz ever find each other again?"

"I'm not going to spoil the story for you!" Celine laughed. "Just keep reading, and I'll make us some food."

Mary frowned. "You've been out working all day, I should have made you some food to come home to, I'm so sorry."

"Don't worry, I remember your cooking, I think I'd rather do it myself thanks."

Mary smiled and sat on a stool by the counter, and continued reading the book. By the time Celine was serving up, Mary had reached the last page. When she closed the book, she felt like she was saying goodbye to a very dear friend. She looked up at Celine, aware that she had tears in her eyes.

"So you think we don't belong because we're not human?" Mary asked.

Celine nodded. "Yes, I think I'm an Angel, and you're a Faerie."

Mary smiled, and felt a rush of warmth through her body at those words. As silly as they sounded, she felt the truth in them. "Yes, I did relate to Aria, actually."

"I thought you might," Celine set down her fork and looked at Mary. "I had booked to go on a retreat, for Earth Angels looking for their Twin Flames, but it was postponed due to the founders of the business passing away. A new couple now run it, and the lady is the author of that book."

Mary nodded, wondering where her sister was going with her words.

"I think you should go instead of me. It's all paid for, you just need to choose the dates you want. There's one coming up, but I've run out of holidays for this year."

"Oh, Celine, I couldn't possibly take your holiday for you! You should go on it, I'm sure they'll let you go next year?"

"But that's just it, I think it didn't happen for a reason. I think you need to go more than I do." Celine smiled. "Consider it your Christmas present for the next few years."

Mary smiled, and tucked into her food with enthusiasm. "Thank you. I really appreciate it."

"I think you can get the bus most of the way, and then they will pick you up from the nearest town. It's kind of in the middle of nowhere, I was planning to drive."

"I'm sure I can work it out." Mary set her fork down and got up from the table. She went over to her sister and hugged her hard. "Thank you for being so amazing. I will repay you for all of this one day."

"Just find your way, that's all the repayment I need," Celine replied.

"I'll do my best."

# Chapter Three

"I'm so pleased you're here, Angel," Violet said as she and Amy made the bed in one of the pods. "I mean, I feel kind of bad that I've roped you into helping out with all of the prep for the retreat, but it's been so great, being able to catch up on everything,"

"Don't feel bad," Amy replied, wrestling a pillow into its case. "I've enjoyed it. And it's been a luxury to sleep in a real bed."

Violet laughed. "Yes the bed in the van isn't the most comfortable in the world, I do remember getting stiff limbs on our travels."

"It's been good to spend time with you both though, and I really do think that you need to find a way to make it together."

Violet sighed. "I know. I'm sure we will."

They finished the bed and Violet smoothed out the wrinkles in the cover. "Sometimes I have no idea how Esmeralda did it all. She used to make it all look so effortless."

"It's because she was an Angel," Amy said seriously.

"Yes," Violet agreed with a smile. "That must be it. I don't think my old soul is cut out for this kind of work."

"You're doing just fine. Now then, what's next?"

They left the pod and headed toward the house. Amy could hear the sounds of an axe chopping wood around the side of the house. She could feel the tension between Violet and Greg, and feared that things may end up the way they did

- 25 -

before. She couldn't bear to see her best friend go through that again.

They went back into the house, and spent the evening sorting out the materials Violet needed for the retreat. Amy picked up a beautifully carved and decorated wooden stick.

"Ah, the talking stick. Most necessary when you get a group of Earth Angels together."

Violet giggled. "Indeed. Though I think I'm the worst culprit for talking over people or cutting in. I swear I just can't help it at times. But having the talking stick definitely helps."

"How many people do you have booked on the course?"

"I haven't checked my email today, but there were five booked in at last count."

"That's good. I'll try not to get in the way too much."

"Don't be silly, you are more than welcome to take part. Though there have only been a few changes to the program since Esmeralda and Mike ran it."

"Thank you, I would enjoy that. Who knows, I might learn more about this mysterious Nick."

Violet frowned. "I hope you haven't been avoiding having relationships with anyone that isn't called Nick."

Amy laughed. "No. I mean, the opportunity for another relationship hasn't really come up since I left Danny, to be honest."

"Good. Because your Flame's name might not be Nick. I would hate to see you missing out or waiting for him and not seeing the perfect guy right in front of you who happens to be called Fred or something."

"I promise that I am not closed off to possibilities. And that I will not focus solely on the name. After all, Greg didn't look the way you imagined he would, did he?"

Violet smiled. "No he didn't. But I know that he is my Flame."

"When do the first guests arrive? Do you want me to do the bus station run?"

"The ones arriving by bus will be arriving in the village at

- 26 -

five, and the rest are coming by car, hopefully before six." Violet pulled her laptop out and checked her email. "Oh good!"

"What?" Amy asked, putting the rest of the oracle cards in order.

"My editor, who I haven't met in person yet, has booked to come on the retreat. I gave her a place on it as a thank you gift for her patience with me while working on the book. She really was an Angel throughout the process. I wasn't sure she would take me up on it though."

"That's great. I started reading the book last night. I love it so far. Which one am I?" Amy teased.

Violet turned to look at her friend. "You are Athena, of course."

Amy smiled, and she found herself blushing. "The head of the Guardian Angels? Really?"

Violet nodded. "I realised that was who you were during the flashback I had here after the meditation we did. I'm sorry I never told you before."

Amy shook her head. "It's okay, I'm just a little blown away. I had no idea I was that important."

Violet got up and embraced her friend. "You are so very important, my dear, sweet Angel. Please remember that."

Amy felt a prickle of tears in her eyes as she hugged her back tightly. It made sense that she and Violet had known each other before, their bond ran so much deeper than just the few years they had known each other.

Amy couldn't wait to read the rest of the book, to find out what happened next.

A few hours later, everything was in place, the food for the evening meal was ready, and they were enjoying a rest before they had to pick up and greet the guests.

Greg came in the door, covered in sawdust and dirt. Violet jumped up to stop him from tracking the dirt everywhere. "Strip by the door and get in the shower," she ordered.

Amy giggled from her spot on the couch, but she didn't

hear Greg's response. She heard clothing fall to the floor, and then footsteps up the stairs. Violet put the clothes straight in the wash and Amy frowned as she heard the washer go on. Usually they would banter and tease each other, but it just seemed so tense over the last couple of days. Amy hoped that once the retreat was over, they would find some time to relax together. She hadn't seen them even take half an hour off to go for a walk.

She smiled at Violet when she re-entered the room, and Violet smiled back, but Amy could see the strain underneath it. Deciding that she needed to do something about the situation, she excused herself to use the bathroom, and went upstairs. She tapped on the main bedroom door, and Greg called out to enter.

She opened the door and poked her head round, hoping that he was decent. She averted her eyes quickly when she saw that he was still only wearing underpants.

"Oh, Amy, um, hang on."

Amy heard the slam of a drawer and the rustle of clothing, and then Greg came over to the door wearing an old pair of jeans and a T-shirt full of holes.

"Sorry," Amy said. "But I just wanted to have a word with you while Violet is busy with her admin stuff."

Greg frowned and gestured for her to enter the room. She perched on the edge of the bed and Greg sat on a chair that was covered in Violet's bright clothing. "Everything okay?" he asked.

"I'm fine. It's you guys I'm worried about. These last few days, it's bothered me how stressed things seem to be. And it feels like it's building up to what happened last time."

Greg looked down at the patterned rug covering the wooden floor and sighed. "I'm afraid of that too. Eighteen months ago, we were at the point of possibly separating again, because I was feeling that perhaps Violet would be better off if we weren't together," he held up his hand when Amy started to cut in. "But we stuck it out, and when Esmeralda passed

- 28 -

away, we ended up here, helping Mike run the place. Then when Mike died too, well, since then, life has just been a series of highs and lows and more stress than I thought was possible." He looked at Amy and sighed. "Violet doesn't laugh as much anymore, and I hate that. We don't have fun together, we're just basically trying to survive each day."

"I can see that. And I know that you two are strong, and that you can make it, but you do need to take time out, for yourselves, and for your relationship. When was the last time you went out for a meal? Or to the cinema? Or just for a walk?"

Greg shook his head. "We haven't don't any of those things much in the last year."

"Right, there's a retreat beginning in an hour, and I will help as much as I can with that, to ease the burden a little, but on Monday, when all the participants leave, I am ordering you both to pack your bags, get in that poor, neglected campervan of yours, and go away for a few days. Go to the seaside, get some fresh air, eat ice cream, stargaze, do whatever it takes to have fun. Do I have your word you will do that? I can take care of this place for a few days."

Greg smiled, and Amy saw his old self for the first time since she'd arrived. "Yes, I can make that happen. Thank you."

Amy leaned over to hug him. "You are most welcome, my friend. Now, I had better go and check on Violet, I think I am on pick up duty."

"I'd better shower and get ready too. I'll be downstairs soon."

"I'll put the kettle on." Amy got up and left the bedroom, pleased that she had done something to help, and feeling a lot less anxious herself. Now that Greg was more relaxed, she was sure that would have a beneficial effect on Violet, and that the weekend would go a lot more smoothly.

*　　*　　*

The closer he got to the village near the retreat, the more Tim's stomach churned with nerves. What was he letting himself in for? He mindlessly followed the monotone commands of the SatNav in the hire car and made his way through the narrow lanes, nearly coming to blows with a tractor, until he finally rattled down the bumpy lane to the retreat. He stared around him in wonder; they really were off the beaten track. He saw the wooden sign for the retreat, pulled into a parking spot, and turned off the engine. The silence that surrounded him was deafening, and he could hear his own heartbeat pounding in his chest. Before he could change his mind, he unbuckled his seatbelt and got out of the car, giving his long legs a good stretch as he went to the boot to remove his small weekend case. He walked down the path, thinking that Aria would love it there, she would just dance among the trees on the fallen leaves. He sighed; he really hoped that the weekend would stop him from thinking about Aria so much. He really wanted to be able to let go.

He reached the front door and rang the bell, and seconds later, the door opened and a familiar face appeared.

"Velvet," he said, unable to stop himself. The woman before him had to be the woman from his memories of the Academy. He had read the book too, and couldn't believe that he was actually mentioned in it.

"Are you Tim?" she asked, holding her hand out. "You're mixing up the book with reality, my name is Violet."

"But you are Velvet, too. I remember."

Violet's eyebrows raised, and she ushered him inside, taking his case for him. He slipped his shoes off and accepted the slippers he was offered.

"You remember being at the Academy?"

Tim nodded. "Yes, and you remember me too, you mentioned me in your book."

"Oh my goodness," Violet's hand flew to her mouth. "Tm? Is that really you? The Starperson?"

"Yes it is," Tim replied with a smile. He held his arms out and Violet hugged him tightly.

"This is incredible," Violet said. "I am so pleased you

have found your way here, Earth Angel! You were the first to leave the last trainee class, and though I knew you must be ready, I was a little worried about you."

Tim pulled away. "There was no need, I have done just fine."

Violet held her hands up. "Indeed you have, please do come in and have a cup of tea. Amy has gone to collect those who were arriving by bus, and we are waiting for another two by car."

"How many of us are there?"

"There will be seven in total, which includes my friend Amy, who will be helping out, but still taking part in the activities."

"Great." Tim followed Violet into the lounge, and she went to the kitchen to put the kettle on.

"Once everyone has arrived, Amy and I will show you to your pods, and then we will have dinner and all get to know each other in an informal way this evening," Violet called out over the noise of the kettle.

"Sounds good." Now that Tim had sat down and relaxed, he felt very sleepy, and while he waited for Violet to make tea, he felt his eyelids drooping.

"Hi, there."

Tim's eyes snapped open and he looked up to see a man in the doorway to the lounge. He got up to greet him.

"I'm Greg," he said, holding his hand out.

Tim shook his hand. "Tim, nice to meet you, Greg."

Greg nodded and headed for the kitchen. Tim heard low voices and then Violet laughing, and he wondered if they were laughing at him. Which was a ridiculous thing to think, but it crossed his mind anyway.

Violet came in with a tray of mugs. Tim took one and settled back on the sofa, and Greg and Violet sat on the other sofa opposite. Before any of them could start a conversation, they heard the bell ringing, and Greg got up to answer the door.

"And so the fun begins," Violet said, smiling at Tim. Her

- 31 -

smile was genuine, and he decided that she couldn't have been laughing at him before. There was a flurry of activity as the other guests arrived, and as Amy arrived back from the bus station with three more. Suddenly the lounge seemed to be very cosy, with everyone squeezed in next to each other, getting to know each other and drinking cups of tea.

Tim sat quietly and drank his cooling tea, feeling a little bit out of his depth. He really didn't do a lot of socialising, and felt a little uncomfortable being the only guy in the room, aside from Greg.

"What was your name? I didn't catch it before."

Tim turned to look at the red-haired woman next to him and smiled. "Tim. What's yours?"

"Joy. Pleased to meet you, Tim."

"That's a beautiful name," Tim commented, starting to relax a little.

Joy smiled. "It's not my given name. I changed it when I was younger because I felt that joy was something I needed more of in my life."

Tim smiled. "I changed my name too. My old name didn't feel right to me somehow."

"So are you excited about this weekend? I've been desperate to attend this retreat since I read Violet's book and found out that this place existed."

"I'm a little bit nervous," Tim said honestly. "I only know about Twin Flames because of my last girlfriend. We were seeing each other for a few months, but she left me for her Flame."

Joy smiled knowingly. "That must have been hard. But at least you know that she didn't leave you because she didn't love you. She only left because it is difficult to resist the lure of the Flame."

Tim leaned in closer as the chatter around them became louder. "How do you know, have you met your Flame?"

Joy shook her head. "Not yet. But I know that I will. I have a few friends who have met their Flames, some of them are

- 32 -

still together, and some of them are in periods of separation. But there is a palpable energy that surrounds them, when they are together. You can feel the electricity in the air. You can see the connection between them. It's quite amazing."

Tim nodded. "I haven't seen anything like that, but I would like to experience it one day."

"I'm sure you will. And I'm sure this weekend will help."

"Okay, is everyone ready to be shown their pods? If you take half an hour to settle in, dinner will be ready by then, just come back to the house and let yourself in, and the tables will be set up in the front room."

Tim and Joy got up with the others, and they all retrieved their bags from the front room and followed Amy, Violet and Greg outside to their homes for the weekend.

When Violet opened the door to his pod and ushered Tim inside, he looked around the simple but beautiful interior and nodded. This weekend was going to shift everything, he could just feel it.

- 34 -

# Chapter Four

"It's beautiful here, isn't it?"

Hannah smiled up at Rachael, who was her pod-mate for the weekend. "It really is," she agreed. "I'm just trying to take it all in. I can't quite believe that we're going to spend the weekend with Violet."

"She's quite amazing, I can tell that her soul is incredibly old. Makes me look young in comparison."

"You're an Old Soul? I was trying to figure out what kind of Earth Angel you were, I assumed you were one."

"Yes, I am an Old Soul," Rachael said, unpacking her small suitcase. "And sometimes I just get so tired, I wonder what I'm doing here. I've been getting signs for a while now that I needed to find out more about the reunion of the Flames, and then an email advertising this retreat just appeared in my inbox."

"How funny, I got that email too, but I hadn't signed up to anything. We should ask Violet about that."

Rachael laughed. "Well I just assumed it was my Guardian Angel behind it, nudging me in the right direction."

Hannah thought of Starlight, and smiled. "You're probably right. I think the Angels were behind it." Hannah put away the few clothes she had brought with her, and got her copy of The Earth Angel Training Academy out of her handbag. "Do you think Violet would sign my copy?"

"I'm sure she would be happy to, she seems really down

- 35 -

to earth."

"Yes, I'm looking forward to learning from her this weekend."

Rachael shook her head and sat next to Hannah. "No, Indigo Child, there is nothing to learn. Only a universe of knowledge to remember."

Hannah frowned. "Have we met before? How did you know I was an Indigo?"

"I could sense it in your aura. The Indigo aura is different to a normal aura. I don't believe we have met before, but then I was at the Academy, so perhaps we did."

"You were? That's incredible. I'm pretty sure I went there too. I have these vague memories of being taught how to be human by two Faeries, which seemed pretty odd to me."

Rachael got up, laughing. She put another jumper over the top of her clothes and shivered a little. "Shall we head back to the house for food? I don't know about you, but I'm really hungry."

Hannah nodded and picked up her book. "Me too. Oh, we should take a torch, it will be dark now."

They made their way through the trees with the help of the mini torch they found in the pod, and headed toward the porch light. Once inside the warm house, they removed their shoes, slipped on the house slippers by the door and hung the torch up, ready to collect on the way back to bed. Four of the others were already sat at the table, chatting away. The small breakfast tables had been pushed together to form one large one. Hannah breathed in the scent of the food appreciatively.

"Smells amazing, doesn't it?" Beatrice asked.

Hannah nodded. "Yeah it does." She and Rachael took their seats, and then the door opened again and Tim arrived.

"Oh good, everyone is here," Violet said, putting a jug of lemon water in the centre of the table. "I'll get Greg to start serving up. Veggie curry and rice okay for everyone?"

There were nods and sounds of agreement all around, and Amy followed Violet out to the kitchen to help her bring the

- 36 -

food in.

Soon, they all had plates of steaming curry in front of them. Hannah reached out to take a naan bread and giggled as Tim tried to take the other side of the same piece.

"Share?" Tim suggested with a smile. She nodded and he tore it in half, offering her the larger piece.

She took it and nibbled on it slowly. She was intrigued by Tim. She hoped he didn't feel too awkward, being the only male in the group.

"So I see Hannah has a copy of the book, has anyone else had a chance to read the Academy? I know Tim has, because he recognised himself in the book as one of the characters. Did anyone else recognise themselves or identify with one of the realms?"

Hannah shyly raised her hand, and Violet smiled at her. "Go ahead, no need to raise your hand."

"I don't know if I am a particular character in the book, but I know I am an Indigo Child. And I just wanted to say, that your description of our world was amazing, and very accurate."

Violet's eyes lit up and Hannah smiled. "Really? That's so incredible to hear. After all, much of the book was channelled, with my own memories as guideposts."

"You really are Velvet, aren't you?" Hannah asked softly. "You have come to take us into the Golden Age?"

"Yes, I am Velvet. And I do really hope so. Though it is not a certain future."

"Certain or not, I'm glad you have not given up." Hannah noticed a small frown appear on Violet's face, and she wondered if she shouldn't have said that. She wasn't sure how much the Old Soul knew of the change in timeline. She carried on eating, and Violet turned to the others.

"Does anyone else have anything to share? Do you all know what kind of Earth Angel you are? I always think that in all relationships and friendships, it's useful to know each other's true origins, so we know how to relate and empathise

- 37 -

with one another."

"I'm a Starperson," Tim offered, when no one else went first.

"Angel," chimed in Amy.

"My sister reckons I'm a Faerie," Mary said quietly. "But I don't know. I did relate to Aria though."

Violet smiled. "Then you may well be a Faerie."

"I'm a Mermaid," Joy said. "I have known most of my life that I was. I cannot be away from the water for too long. Even just being here in the woods for the weekend, is a challenge for me."

"There is a river nearby, we shall visit it during one of our walks."

Joy nodded enthusiastically. "Sounds good."

"I'm an Old Soul," Rachel said, as they all turned to her. "I'm pretty sure I was at the Academy too, I recognised it from the description."

"Beatrice, what about you?" Violet asked her editor.

Beatrice looked up from her food and shrugged. "I don't know, I think maybe an Angel, but I'm not a hundred percent sure."

"I thought you were an Angel. I never told you this before, because I wasn't certain, but now we have met, I think it's true."

"What is?" Beatrice asked.

"I think you are Beryl. And that you worked with me at the Academy."

Beatrice's eyebrows raised in surprise. "Really?"

Violet nodded. "Yes. Without you, I couldn't have got the book about the Academy finished and ready for the world. And I know from my memories that I couldn't have run the Academy without Beryl."

Tears spilled down Beatrice's face, and Hannah reached out to hug her, wanting to comfort the Angel.

Beatrice smiled through her tears. "Knowing that makes me feel comforted," she whispered. "Thank you."

- 38 -

"Thank you, my dear Angel. I'm so pleased we were able to find each other again." Violet wiped away a tear of her own, and then picked up her wine glass.

"I would like to propose a toast, to a most magical and wonderful weekend together, here at the Twin Flame Retreat."

Everyone picked up their glasses and clinked them against each other's.

"And I would also like to make a toast to Greg, my Twin Flame, for this incredible curry."

Hannah giggled and raised her glass again with the others, while Greg shrugged and looked embarrassed at the attention. To deflect the praise, he leaned over and kissed Violet, catching her by surprise. Hannah averted her gaze from the couple and looked up to see Tim watching her intently. She smiled shyly at him and continued eating her meal.

*       *       *

It had been difficult to not drink any alcohol during the meal, and Mary was now regretting her abstinence as she tried to fall asleep. She still wasn't quite sure why she had come. So far, everyone seemed lovely, and being in the woods made her feel very much at home, but somehow, it all just seemed a little too unreal for her. To believe that Angels and Faeries and aliens were actually real, seemed as crazy as believing that vampires and werewolves were real, which was ridiculous.

She jumped then, when she heard a low howling noise outside.

"Was that a wolf?" Beatrice's frightened voice stage-whispered.

"Surely not," Mary responded. "I don't think there are wolves in this area. Or even wild in the UK. It's probably a dog." Beatrice's evident fear made her feel a little bolder, but her own heart was hammering in her ears.

"Are you sure?" Beatrice asked.

"Yes, I am," Mary lied, to make her feel better. "Positive."

"Okay, thank you."

Mary was quiet for a while, and soon she heard Beatrice's breathing deepen and figured she must have gone to sleep. She wondered if it would be possible to sneak into the house and get some alcohol. She was sweating and craving it. How she thought she could just quit, she wasn't sure.

Unable to take it anymore, she slipped out of bed, threw a jumper over her pyjamas and shoved her feet into her trainers, then nabbed the mini torch and slipped out of the pod quietly. As soon as she stepped outside, her fear that there might be a wolf out there returned and she gasped. She looked around wildly, but everything was still, there wasn't even a breath of wind through the trees. Before she could chicken out and go back into the pod, she walked quickly down the path, pleased that the moonlight was so bright through the trees. She reached the house and found the hiding place where the key was. Violet had told them where it was so they could go in to use the bathroom in the night if they needed to.

She opened the door as quietly as possible, and removed her trainers. She tiptoed through the front room into the lounge, and then into the kitchen, thanking the Angels again for the bright moon lighting her way through the windows.

She opened the fridge and spotted the half full bottle of white wine. She pulled it out and closed the door.

"Couldn't sleep?"

Mary jumped and the bottle slipped out of her hand, shattering on the stone floor with a deafening crash.

The light flicked on then, and Mary looked up to see Greg. Her face paled. "I'm so sorry," she whispered. "I just, I just," her face fell and a sob escaped. "I'm sorry."

She felt a hand on her arm, and looked up to look at Greg.

"Don't worry about it. Just stay there while I sweep up the glass, I don't want you to step on the glass in your socks, okay?"

Mary nodded. He got the dustpan and brush, and swept up around her feet, before wiping up the sticky wine.

- 40 -

Mary just watched him silently, tears streaming down her cheeks. Was it not enough that her addictive behaviour had landed her in hospital? Now she was stealing alcohol from stranger's fridges?

Once Greg was satisfied there was no more glass on the floor, he guided her over to a stool, and she sat down while he made them a cup of tea.

He set the cups down on the breakfast counter and sat on a stool next to her. "I'm sorry I startled you; that wasn't my intention."

Mary shook her head. "I'm sorry I was trying to steal the wine."

Greg chuckled, taking her by surprise. "It's not stealing. It was available at dinnertime. If you had wanted more, you could have just had it."

Mary sipped her tea. "I didn't have any at dinner. I haven't had any alcohol for a week."

Realisation dawned on Greg's face and he nodded. "I see. Giving up?"

Mary nodded. "I ended up in hospital last week after a night out. I don't even remember what happened, but apparently a bouncer stopped some random man from taking me home with him."

Greg didn't respond, and just sipped his tea, allowing her to spill out everything that no one but her sister knew.

"I've just been finding it hard, to exist in this world. To be here. Drinking and taking drugs is how I escape. Sometimes I have the most amazing hallucinations, but mostly, it just blocks everything out, just makes it all go away."

"I think there are a lot of Earth Angels who feel the same way. That they don't want to be here. And there are many that choose to go home, rather than stick it out, because it is not easy being human in these times."

Mary nodded in agreement. "So what about the ones who choose to stay? How do they cope?"

"Lots of different ways. I think entering a more spiritual

- 41 -

way of life can help. And different practices like meditation, or healing can also help. But there are many healthy ways to find peace. Walking, running, writing, painting, making love," Greg smiled and Mary blushed.

"It's about finding beauty in ordinary things. Really noticing the world around you. It's difficult at times, to see the good when the bad is shouting in our faces, but it can be done. And it's even easier to do in this kind of environment. Just watching a leaf falling from a tree, a bird building its nest or feeling the rain on your face can cleanse your soul of the darkness."

Mary smiled. "Even listening to you talk about it makes me feel better."

Greg smiled back. "Would you like to go for a walk? It might help you sleep."

"Are there wolves in the area?" Mary asked without thinking.

Greg laughed and shook his head. "No, that will be Kahn, our next door neighbour's dog. He likes to think he's a wolf and howls at the moon occasionally. It does freak people out sometimes."

Mary giggled in relief. "In that case, I'd love to go for a walk."

Greg hopped off the stool and set their mugs by the sink. Mary glanced at the clock and saw it was just after midnight. She appreciated Greg taking the time to make her feel better. She didn't think this was part of the course.

She followed him to the door, put her shoes on and picked up her torch. Once outside, they walked down the driveway, their way lit by the moon. She didn't need to switch the torch on.

"We won't go far," Greg whispered. "There's just a place I think you would like. It looks amazing in the moonlight."

"Okay," Mary whispered back. She walked alongside Greg through the woods, and his words from earlier filtered through her mind. She looked around her, appreciating the

- 42 -

magic and the beauty of the moonlit scenery surrounding her. Instead of being scared by noises she didn't recognise, she listened closely, trying to identify them.

"That's an owl," Greg whispered. "It visits often with its young."

Mary smiled, feeling safe with him walking beside her. After a few minutes, they reached a small clearing in the trees.

"This is where I come when I need to think," Greg said. He laid out a blanket on the ground and he sat down on it, patting the space beside him. She sat next to him, and when he lay back, she did the same. Despite the bright moonlight, the number of stars she could see blew her mind. Where she lived, there was just too much light pollution to be able to see any stars. The night skies were permanently stained orange by the streetlamps.

"It's so beautiful," Mary said.

"Yes," Greg agreed. "I feel it puts everything into perspective."

Mary was quiet then. She watched the stars, and breathed in the cool air. She tried to really open herself up to the beauty of the present moment, and let go of all that had come before. Amazingly, in that moment, even her cravings and need for alcohol and other substances disappeared. She didn't want to escape anymore, she just wanted the moment to last forever.

"Nothing lasts forever," Greg whispered.

# Chapter Five

"Did you sleep well?"

Beatrice looked up and nodded at Tim. "Yes, once I had got used to the noises and was assured there were no wolves in the UK."

Tim chuckled. "Yes, I heard that too, I think it was a dog."

"Oh no, was Kahn howling again?" Violet asked as she set their breakfast in front of them. "I am sorry, I should have warned you. I forget that people aren't used to the countryside noises. Though admittedly, Kahn's howling isn't exactly typical noise."

Beatrice laughed. "It's okay, Mary was very reassuring."

Mary looked up at the sound of her name and smiled. Beatrice thought she looked different this morning and that something about her had changed. She would have to ask her about it later.

Beatrice tucked into her muesli with enthusiasm, she had already been for a short run that morning, and was now feeling quite ravenous. It was a different experience, running through the woods instead of through the streets of the town she lived in. It was a refreshing change; she vowed to try and find woodlands near where she lived to run in the future.

"When everyone has had enough to eat and drink, please make your way to the tent in the garden, for our first activity of the weekend. I'm going to get set up, if you need anything else, just ask Amy or Greg." Everyone nodded and Violet made her way out the house after giving Greg a quick kiss.

Beatrice watched her go, and thought about what she'd said, about her being Beryl. It did resonate, somehow, that she had been her. It would be interesting to see if anything came up over the weekend. Beatrice still felt a little trepidation at the idea of the meditations and workshops. She still wasn't really sure she actually believed in the whole Twin Flame concept, but after seeing Violet and Greg together, it seemed a little more likely. There definitely was something about their relationship that was different to other relationships that Beatrice had seen and experienced.

She knew that the characters of Velvet and Laguz were based on them, and she wondered if everything that Violet had included in the book about their history together had actually happened.

She blinked and reminded herself to chew her mouthful of muesli. It all still blew her mind a little. When she had initially read the book and agreed to edit it, she thought she was dealing with a fantasy novel. When she had got to know Violet a little better through several long phone calls, she had admitted to Beatrice that there was a lot of truth in the book, and the rest that Violet didn't know consciously was channelled.

"I'm going out to the tent," Tim said, breaking Beatrice out of her thoughts.

She smiled at him and drank the last gulp of tea. She stood up. "I'll come with you."

Tim nodded and they headed out of the door, following Rachael and Hannah. Mary and Joy were still eating.

"We'll be there in a minute," Joy said, waving her spoon.

"Yeah me too," Amy said, clearing away the plates.

Beatrice nodded and followed the others. They went down the woodchip path to the tent. Beatrice hadn't seen inside the tent yet, but from the pictures on the website, she knew it would look amazing.

She ducked through the door, and removed her shoes in the awning with the others, then they stepped into the white tent in their socks. It was like being inside a cloud. The floors were soft and cushioned, and there were blankets and pillows laid out in a circle, and swathes of white fabric covering the ceiling and the sides, reminding Beatrice of the inside of a circus tent, not that she'd ever been in one in real life.

Beatrice settled on a pillow next to Mary, and then Tim settled on the pillow next to her. She sat cross-legged, and closed her eyes, breathing deeply.

"You look like you've done this before," Tim whispered.

She smiled and looked at him. "I've done some yoga classes. I'm a bit of a fitness freak, it makes up for the fact that I spend so many hours sat in front of my computer."

Tim nodded. "I hear you. I really should do more exercise. The most I do is walking to and from work."

"I find it calms me, soothes my nerves after dealing with irate clients all day."

"Editing is your full-time job?"

"Yes, I work from home now, I used to work in a publishing house, but after a few years I felt like I wanted to strike out on my own, make my own hours. And so far, it's working well, I have a decent number of clients, and I enjoy the work mostly. It's just that I occasionally have to edit things I would rather not, like the history of a town no one has ever heard of, or really bad erotic novels."

Tim laughed. "I can imagine that would be difficult. Can't you just set the submission requirements so you only accept work in a certain genre?"

Beatrice sighed. "That's my goal, but at the moment, I'm trying to build up my portfolio and client list. It was a bit of a leap, going from full-time well-paid employment to working for myself, and I suppose I still don't quite have the confidence that enough work will keep coming in so I can pay my bills and mortgage."

"It will happen," Tim assured her. "Are you going to edit Violet's next book?"

"Am I writing another book?" Violet asked, joining their

conversation.

Beatrice and Tim looked up at the Old Soul, and realised that everyone was sitting quietly, waiting for the meditation to start.

"I hope so," Tim said, seemingly oblivious to Beatrice's embarrassment. "I really enjoyed the first one. I'd love to know what happens next."

Violet smiled. "We will have to wait and see. Now then, is everyone ready?"

"Is Greg not joining us?" Mary asked.

"He's getting ready for the workshop this afternoon. We tend to switch between us on these weekends, so we're not on the go continuously. While you are with him the afternoon, I will be organising dinner and the evening activity."

Mary nodded and settled onto her cushion.

"This first meditation is just a way to relax, to enter your subconscious and to possibly re-visit a time in a past life where you were with your Twin Flame. Just listen to my voice and close your eyes, and we'll go on this journey together."

Beatrice closed her eyes, and felt the heat in her cheeks receding. She breathed deeply and listened to Violet's voice.

\*     \*     \*

Hannah stood in front of the door bearing her name, and smiled at the golden plaque shining on the indigo blue door. She took a deep breath and stepped through. She hadn't voiced any of her fears that Indigos didn't have Twin Flames. So she had no idea what she would find on the other side of the door.

As soon as she stepped through, she looked around and smiled. She was in the Earth Angel Training Academy, in the room with the Rainbows. Having just read about the Rainbows in Violet's book, she wondered if it was just her imagination creating this scene, or whether it was actually a memory from her previous lifetime.

She stepped into the midst of the dancing Rainbows and

held her hand out to catch one. She closed her hand around the tiny light and heard a beautiful voice, making her shiver.

"Dear Indigo! We are so pleased you have come to visit us."

"I need your advice, Rainbows," Hannah said. "I want to know if I will meet my Twin Flame, when I am human."

"Though we are reluctant to predict the future, as we believe that the joy of being human is the uncertainty and unpredictability of life, we want to reassure you, before you leave for your mission. So yes, dear Indigo, you will indeed meet your Twin. You have never had a lifetime together before, this will be the first time you have met, though as we are all connected, throughout the whole universe, you will of course know each other well."

"Thank you, Rainbows, you have made me feel much better. Though I am also worried that I will lose my connection to my siblings when I am on Earth, what can I do to remain connected to them?"

"When you are on Earth, a deep, indigo blue stone will come into your possession, and when worn or held, it will reconnect you to the Indigo web when you feel like you have become disconnected. Do not seek out the stone, it will find you."

Hannah nodded, and felt she could let go of the colourful light beam. She opened her hand and watched it dance away to re-join the others. "Thank you, Rainbows, I look forward to seeing you again when you get to Earth."

She turned away from the Rainbows and stepped back through the door. For a moment, she expected to be in the white hallways of the Academy, but of course found herself in the corridor of doors again. Just as she was considering checking out what was through Rachael's door, it opened and Rachael came out.

"Oh!" Hannah said. "This is weird. I'm sorry, I was just curious."

Rachael chuckled. "That's okay, a little curiosity can be

- 49 -

good. I just got the feeling Violet would be calling us back soon, so I left."

With that, they both heard a voice and looked up.

"If you haven't already gone back through the door to the corridor, please do so now, and make your way outside."

Rachael smiled at Hannah. "See? My intuition rarely steers me wrong. Let's head out."

Hannah followed Rachael, and listened to Violet's voice guiding them back down the path to their current reality.

"Now, you are going to go up the steps, and I will count down each one until you reach the top, and become aware of your body again."

Hannah went up the steps, and slowly became aware of her limbs, of the pillow beneath her, and the sound of the trees rustling outside the tent.

She opened her eyes when Violet got to the tenth step, and she looked across at Rachael in amazement. Had they really just shared consciousness?

Rachael winked back at her, and Violet opened up the floor for them to share their experiences of the meditation with each other.

# Chapter Six

"I was in this weird place, that looked like it was underwater, but there was no water. Everything was moving like it was being pulled around by an invisible current. There were even fish floating past." Mary looked around the others, aware that what she spoke of sounded completely insane. But they were just nodding and smiling back at her.

"I was in this place, and there was a Merman swimming along, and when he saw me, he smiled, and asked if I was okay. And I realised then that I felt very upset. So I shook my head and he took me by the hand to sit on a large rock with him, I seemed to be floating along too, or maybe I was flying. When our hands touched, it was like I'd had an electric shock." Mary shook her head, still not believing she was actually recounting what sounded as insane as her nightly dreams. "Lucky there wasn't any water really."

The others chuckled.

"Do you remember speaking to him?" Violet asked softly.

Mary nodded. "Yes, he asked me what was wrong, and I told him that I felt really lonely. I had left my family behind when I'd come to the Academy, and I missed them. I had made friends but I didn't feel like I belonged there." Mary smiled. "He just put his arm around me and said that no one belonged there, and that what we had signed up to do was not an easy task, and that when we got to Earth, we would feel even more disconnected, but that if we found the one, our Flame, then we

- 51 -

would be home, no matter where we were."

Her smiled disappeared. She had felt so loved in his embrace, it had been difficult to leave him there, and come back to reality.

"Was he your Flame?" Joy whispered. "The Merman?"

Mary looked at her, her eyes wide. She hadn't even thought to ask him that. But considering how she'd felt when their hands had touched, it wouldn't surprise her if he was. "I think he might just be, yes."

There were sighs around the room, and Mary felt tears welling up in her eyes. As if sensing how lost she felt in that moment, Amy scooted closer to her and wrapped her arms around her in a beautiful hug. Mary closed her eyes and hid her face in the Incarnated Angel's shoulder and felt a little less lonely.

"This meditation can bring up a lot of emotions, and that's a good thing. Sometimes, the only reason that Earth Angels have not yet met their Flames, is because they have shut down and closed themselves off from the possibility. This meditation was created for you to access your sometimes ancient memories when you were with your Flame, so that your hearts are opened to meeting them now."

Mary looked up from Amy's shoulder at Violet and nodded. "I feel a bit raw and exposed."

"Greg will be leading some healing work this afternoon, which will enable you to heal any past trauma that is associated with your Flame, and he will help you to be open-hearted, and to be able to love unconditionally again, but still protect yourselves from lower vibrational energies that will drag you down and take you off course."

"Sounds good," Joy said. "I could definitely use some healing like that."

Violet smiled. "Now then, who would like to share their experience next?"

\*     \*     \*

- 52 -

He was hungry, but Tim found it difficult to eat the lunch that Greg had made them for when they emerged from the tent around twelve o clock. He dipped his bread into the soup and chewed on the soggy corner, his mind whirling.

He hadn't shared his meditation story with the others, because it had seemed too weird. Even more so than Mary's underwater scene that had no water and Hannah's room full of rainbows. When he had stepped through the door bearing his name, he had become formless, and had felt so free, and so at home. He had visited a place that was so familiar to him, yet impossible to describe at the same time. He just had this overwhelming feeling of peace and connection and sense of belonging. He felt as though he had communicated with other beings, but it wasn't something he was able to translate in any way into English so that the others in the group could understand it.

All he knew, was that when he was called back to the door, and he stepped out into the corridor as a human again, he had felt utterly lost. Like he had been ripped away from his home, his haven, his safe place, and had been dumped in the middle of hell. It had taken all his willpower to not just start crying when he opened his eyes and found himself on Earth again.

"Are you okay?"

Tim blinked and focused on Rachael, who was sat across from him and peering at him in concern. He realised then that he had been staring into space and had forgotten the rest of the bread in his raised hand.

He nodded and dunked the remaining bread in his soup, which broke off, causing him to need his spoon to fish it out.

"If you want to talk about what happened this morning, then please feel that you can. This is probably the least judgemental group of people you will ever find."

Tim smiled. "Thank you. It's not that I didn't want to share it, it was more that I couldn't find a way to express it in words. I'm pretty sure I went home, to my own planet, where there is no form, or words or anything, other than feelings and knowingness. So it's difficult to really describe what happened there."

"But you were sad to come back."

Tim bowed his head, and willed himself not to show how upset he was, he didn't do public displays of emotion. "Yes." After a few moments of silence, Tim looked back up to see that Rachael had continued to eat her lunch, and seemed to understand that he didn't want to be questioned further.

He finished his soup, interested to see what would happen in the afternoon healing session with Greg. Perhaps it would help him to figure out what had happened during the meditation. He wiped his mouth with his napkin and glanced at his watch. He had ten minutes before the next session was to begin, and he wanted to go back to his pod to grab another jumper. He had felt quite cold during the morning session, despite the cosiness of the tent.

He excused himself from the table, and then slipped his shoes back on and left the house. He walked down the path toward the pods, and as he looked up at the trees he suddenly realised that he hadn't thought about Aria since he'd arrived, which had to be a positive step forward.

He reached his pod, stepped inside, and dug a thicker jumper out of his case. He pulled it on and then set off back toward the house. The healing was taking place in the workshop room upstairs.

"Hey, mind if I walk with you?"

Tim looked up to see Hannah leaving her pod and smiled. He nodded and she fell in step with him.

"How are you finding it so far? This morning was pretty crazy wasn't it?"

"Yeah, it was. I don't know what to make of it all yet, but I'm looking forward to this afternoon."

"Me, too." Hannah stopped suddenly and put her arm out to stop Tim too. "Look," she whispered.

He followed her line of sight and saw a deer through the trees, just a few yards away from them. The deer watched them for a few moments, then continued on her way. Hannah gasped with delight as a tiny baby deer followed close behind her.

They both watched until they could no longer see the mother and baby, then Hannah turned to Tim, a smile lighting up her whole face. "Wasn't that just magical?"

He nodded. "Yes, it was." In that moment, he had a sudden and unexpected urge to kiss her. He blinked and turned away, and they carried on walking toward the house. Tim glanced sideways at Hannah, hoping she hadn't noticed his weird reaction.

They re-entered the house and made their way upstairs to the workshop room. The others were already there, making themselves comfortable in the unusual space. Tim looked around, appreciating the structure and décor of the room, it was very otherworldly, which made him feel quite at home.

"Everyone fed and watered and comfortable?" Greg asked as Tim and Hannah settled down into the circle.

They all nodded and Greg smiled. "Great, to begin with, we're just going to get relaxed and do a short tuning-in process, then I will work around the group with each of you, figuring out what emotions are trapped and need releasing, then we will do a letting go process as a group. The emotions will not be named out loud or discussed, and they don't need to be for them to be released."

"Isn't it good for us to know what we are letting go of?" Mary asked. "Because what if we're not ready to let it go?"

"I will specifically ask for the emotion that is a priority to be released, that will help you move on to the next step. If you really want to know what the emotion is, I can discuss it with you later, but it is sometimes good to just let it go without bringing it into the conscious mind."

Mary nodded, looking reassured, but still a little wary.

"Any other questions before we begin? Once we have let go, I will lead a healing meditation, at which point you may want to lay down and make yourself comfortable - it's quite likely that you will need to sleep afterwards, and if you are still asleep when dinner is ready, I will come up and use a vibroacoustic method to bring you back into this world again."

Tim saw Mary's eyes widen in fear and Amy reached across and patted her hand. "Don't worry," she whispered. "You're in a safe space. If you feel really uncomfortable at any point, just let me know."

Mary smiled at Amy and nodded, then Greg began the tuning-in process, using tuning forks at different vibrations.

Tim closed his eyes and allowed himself to relax, and focus entirely on the sounds, ignoring the fact that he could sense the heat of Hannah's body sitting so close to his.

# Chapter Seven

When Amy opened her eyes, for a moment she had no idea where she was. She blinked a few times to focus, and became aware of her body. She looked around, but the room was very dark and it was difficult to make out any shapes or outlines that would orientate her.

She sat up and finally remembered that she was in the workshop room at the retreat and they had just released trapped emotions. She must have fallen into a deep sleep after the healing, because she had trouble remembering exactly what happened.

She stretched, and as her eyesight adjusted to the gloom she could see that everyone else was still asleep. She quietly and carefully got up and tiptoed around the sleeping bodies to the door, and then slipped through the fabric opening into the corridor. She blinked and adjusted to the light in the corridor and then yawned. What had Greg done to them all?

She made her way downstairs, and could smell Violet's cooking. She headed for the kitchen, and found Violet and Greg in deep conversation. She stopped and watched them for a moment, and smiled when Greg said something in Violet's ear and she giggled softly. They looked more like their old selves again, and Amy was pleased. She was still going to hold Greg to taking Violet away for a few days though. They needed a break.

She cleared her throat to make herself known, and they

both looked up.

"Amy! You've resurfaced. Let me get you a cup of tea," Greg said, jumping up and putting the kettle on.

"Thanks," Amy said, yawning and settling onto one of the barstools. "What happened up there? What time is it?"

Violet glanced at the cooker. "It's nearly seven. Greg will wake everyone else up in a minute, because food is nearly ready."

"Seven! How long have we all been asleep?"

"About three hours," Greg said, setting a steaming cup of tea in front of Amy. She smiled up at him in thanks, and wrapped her hands around it.

"Amazing. Seriously, what happened? What did you do?"

Greg smiled. "Exactly what I said I would. I identified and released trapped emotions that were no longer serving you."

"Why does it knock you out though?"

Greg tilted his head to one side and thought for a moment. "I think it's because your body and aura has to adjust to not having that emotion anymore, and while your body reset itself, the brain needs to be in a sleep-like state." He shrugged. "That's my own view, if you have any other ideas I'd be open to hearing them. After I did the training course for the therapy, I slept for a whole twenty-four hours while my body adjusted to all of the emotions I had released during the training itself."

"Well, your body probably had a lot of trapped emotions that weren't even yours," Amy said, sipping her tea. Though she didn't know the whole story, Amy knew that Greg had been a walk-in, and had taken over the body that he currently had, from a soul who no longer wanted to remain on Earth.

"It's true," Greg agreed. "I just know that I felt much lighter afterwards."

"You have been different since you did that training," Violet commented as she checked on the veggies roasting in the oven.

"In a good way, I hope," Greg teased.

"Yes, honey," Violet said, going over to him and kissing

the back of his neck. "Definitely for the better. Now, do you think you could go and wake up our guests so I can feed them please?"

"Yes, ma'am," Greg said jokingly. He got up and headed for the stairs.

"You guys seem happier than yesterday," Amy commented after he'd left.

Violet smiled. "Yes, it's weird, but something shifted yesterday, and I feel much more relaxed now, despite the fact that we're running about doing the retreat."

"That's great, I'm glad to hear it. You were worrying me with that talk of splitting up."

Violet sighed. "It doesn't thrill me to talk about it or even think about it either, but hopefully we will be able to work it all out."

"I hope so too."

They heard footsteps on the stairs then, and Violet smiled at Amy. "Ready to help me serve the newly regenerated Earth Angels?"

"Absolutely." Amy jumped up and got the plates out of the cupboard, and then Violet got the veggies and nut roast out of the oven and started to serve up. Amy took the first two plates out to the front room, and set them down in front of a very sleepy Joy and Rachael.

"You okay guys?"

Joy nodded. "That was just so strange, what happened?"

Amy laughed. "I asked the exact same thing. Apparently we have released all the negative emotions that we no longer need. Which will hopefully mean that we will be in a better place to meet our Flames."

Rachael yawned and picked up her fork. "This looks amazing, I'm starving. I feel like my entire being has been reconfigured."

"Me too," Mary chimed in as she sat down at a table.

Amy went to get the next two plates, and when everyone was seated and served, she sat down with her own food, opposite Hannah.

"How are you feeling?" she asked the Indigo.

Hannah shook her head. "It's strange, but I feel like I've been home, to my planet, this afternoon. I remember visiting the golden city, seeing my siblings again, and taking part in a meeting."

Amy's eyes widened. "Wow, that's incredible. Do you remember what happened in the meeting?"

Hannah shook her head. "No, but perhaps it's within my subconscious still." She glanced across the table to where Tim sat, and Amy saw them lock gazes for a moment. She frowned. She knew that gaze, she had seen it on the faces of Violet and Greg enough times.

Before she could analyse it further, Hannah looked away and continued eating.

"Is everybody up for watching a movie tonight?" Violet asked. "I thought it would be a good idea to do something relaxing."

There were nods of agreement all round, and then silence as everyone concentrated on eating their food.

As Amy ate, her mind drifted and she wondered how long it would be before she met her own Twin Flame, Nick. She hoped it wouldn't be long, she wanted to experience the kind of unconditional love she had witnessed over the last couple of years. She frowned again as she realised that her fear of finding her Twin Flame, only to lose him again, had completely disappeared. She went within for a moment, and could almost sense the gap where it used to exist. Was that what she had let go of that afternoon?

She looked up and caught Greg looking at her. She smiled at him and he nodded back.

\*     \*     \*

Beatrice couldn't concentrate on the moving images on the screen, they were meaningless shapes and sounds to her.

She shifted about on the cushion and reached out to grab another homemade cookie from the plate resting in-between them all. She loved having food cooked for her, making meals for one got very boring after a while, and Violet and Greg's homemade cooking and baking was amazing.

She ate the cookie slowly, savouring the taste, and gave up trying to make sense of the movie they were watching. She thought about the healing session that afternoon. Though it didn't seem possible, suddenly, when she awoke, she felt ready to meet her Flame, and her fears of not finding someone because she was unable to have a family had gone. She knew that she would find a man who wasn't worried about that, and loved her madly anyway.

Her heart thumped suddenly at the idea of finding the one she was supposed to be with. To experience the kind of love and connection that she had read about in Violet's book.

She also noticed that she felt less sceptical about the whole concept. That she believed, wholeheartedly, that her Flame not only existed, but that she would meet him soon. She shook her head. Whatever Greg had done must have been pretty powerful.

The movie ended and Beatrice still had no idea what it had been about. She sleepily stretched and said good night to everyone, before heading back to the pod she was sharing with Mary.

"Wasn't that a great movie?" Mary asked as they changed into their pyjamas.

Beatrice blushed. "I didn't actually take any of it in to be honest, I was in my own little world."

Mary giggled. "That's cool. I was a little spaced out too, after this afternoon. I had no idea what to expect from this weekend, but it's been amazing so far." She dove into bed and snuggled up under the covers.

Beatrice got into her own bed and looked over at the Faerie. "I know we only met yesterday, but I have to say, you seem different already."

Mary nodded. "I feel different. But at the same time, I feel more like myself."

Beatrice smiled. "That sounds great. I was just thinking earlier that I feel less fearful, and less negative about meeting my Flame."

"That sounds good too," Mary said sleepily. She closed her eyes, and within seconds, was breathing deeply. Beatrice reached out and switched off the lamp on the table between their beds. She lay in the dark pod, staring into the nothingness, and wondered what the next day would bring.

# Chapter Eight

Hannah walked through the house, moving from room to room, taking note of the décor and the furniture. She saw lots of photo frames everywhere, but the images they contained were too fuzzy for her to recognise the faces. When directed, she went outside to dig up a box in the garden. She picked up the shovel and started digging, pleased when she felt a metallic resistance. She set the shovel aside and knelt down to reach into the hole. But before she could open the ornate box, a hand on her arm made her jump and look up.

"Starlight!" she said, relieved to see it was just her friend. "What are you doing here?"

Starlight knelt down next to her. "I'm just making sure that you are ready for what you are about to find. Because once you open that box, there will be no going back. Your life will change forever, and you will have to work hard to stay on course with your mission. Are you ready?"

Hannah frowned at the serious tone in her friend's voice. She looked down at the box, which was a dark blue metal, with a golden trim and hinges. She was ready. She didn't expect the path ahead to be smooth and easy. She was ready to meet her Flame, and to meet all the challenges that came with that.

"I'm ready," she whispered.

Starlight nodded and stood up. "Then I wish you well, my dear Indigo. Remember that I am here for you whenever you need me."

Hannah nodded and Starlight disappeared. She looked down at the box again then slowly opened it. Nestled inside, was a dark blue crystal, which gleamed in the sunlight. She took it out of the box and examined it. It looked like the stone that the Rainbows had described. But how was this going to change her life forever? It still didn't give her any clues as to who her Flame was, or how she was going to find him. She looked in the box again, but there was nothing else in there.

"Now close the box, and replace it in the ground, then leave the garden through the front gate, and make your way back down the path."

Hannah followed Violet's instructions, choosing to put the blue stone in her pocket. A few minutes later, when Violet had brought them all back to the present moment, she opened her eyes and noticed that Tim was staring at her, a weird look on his face. She smiled at him, but his expression didn't change, making her frown a little.

"Did everyone find something in their box? Would anyone like to share?" Violet asked.

Mary put her hand up shyly and Violet nodded to her. "I found a map in mine. A map of Ireland."

"Did that mean anything to you?" Violet asked.

Mary shook her head. "Not really, I've never been to Ireland. But there was a place name on the map, circled in red. It was a coastal town called Ardmore." She shrugged. "I've never even heard of it before, what do you think it means?"

Violet smiled. "A few years ago, I did this same meditation with Esmeralda, the Angel who used to run this retreat, and I found a place name in my box too. A few months later, I went there, to that place, which was in France. I was walking along the beach, and decided to climb some rocks to photograph the sunrise, but I fell into the water."

There were a few gasps around the room, and Hannah's heart skipped a beat.

"I was knocked unconscious, and when I was revived, I realised I had been saved by none other than my Twin Flame."

- 64 -

She smiled and looked at each of them in turn. "I know it sounds like a crazy story, and I wouldn't recommend falling into the sea so your Flame can rescue you. I also broke my leg in the fall, and to this day, it's painful when the weather gets colder."

"So you think I should go there? To Ardmore?" Mary asked.

"If that feels like the right thing to do, then yes. I was unsure of going to France, it was Amy who encouraged me," she looked at her best friend who smiled back. "And I am very glad that I did it. The information in the box is a message from your Guardian Angel. They wish for you to meet your Flame, for you to experience the incredible connection and unconditional love."

"What if the contents of the box doesn't give you any clues at all?" Hannah found herself asking.

"May I ask what was in the box?" Violet asked.

"It was a small, deep blue crystal. I don't know what it was called though."

"Hmm, it could be Lapis Lazuli, perhaps, or maybe sodalite?" Violet mused.

"Was it this?"

Hannah looked up at Tim, who was holding his hand out to her across the circle. She held out her hand and he dropped a blue crystal onto her palm. She looked at it closely. It was identical to the one in her box.

She looked up at Tim, her eyes wide.

"It's iolite," he said softly. "I've had it for years, I always carry it in my pocket, but I've never told anyone, or shown it to anyone before."

Hannah was oblivious to everyone in the tent other than Tim in that moment. "The Rainbows told me that to stay connected to my fellow Indigos, a blue stone would come into my possession. They told me this after I asked them about my Flame, who they said I had not had a life with before, but would know well when I met them."

"Tim," Violet said softly. "What was in your box?"

Tim didn't take his gaze from Hannah's as he answered the Old Soul. "It was a photo in a blue frame. It was quite dusty, so I wiped the glass with my t-shirt and realised it contained a picture of me. And you were next to me."

Hannah gasped. The framed photos from her meditation suddenly came into sharp focus in her mind. "Was I wearing a green top with black hearts on it? And you were wearing a black t-shirt with a logo here?" She gestured to the middle of her chest.

Tim nodded, his eyes wide.

"I saw that photo too, in my house in the meditation." She looked down at the crystal in her hand, which felt like it was glowing red hot. Then she looked up at Tim again, not knowing what to say.

"I think perhaps we should go in for lunch," Violet said softly. "Hannah, Tim, if you would like to stay here a bit longer, you are most welcome."

Hannah was only vaguely aware of the movement of the others, and the cool breeze as they left the tent. When they were alone, Tim moved closer to her and he wrapped his hands around hers, around the crystal. Her hands tingled at his touch, and her heart thudded heavily. Was he really her Flame?

"Are you really my Flame?" Tim whispered, echoing her thoughts, a hopeful look on his face.

"I don't know," Hannah answered honestly. "If we've never met before, how do we tell whether we are or not?"

"May I kiss you?" Tim asked.

Hannah smiled. "Do you think that will help?" she teased.

"Yes, I do."

Hannah leaned forward and Tim met her halfway. When their lips met, Hannah felt as though she was suddenly hurtling through the universe at top speed, with stars, planets and galaxies flying past her.

\*   \*   \*

He was home.

When his lips met Hannah's, he was transported suddenly to his own planet, where everything made sense, where he knew he belonged, where he felt loved, unconditionally.

Reluctantly, after what felt like an eternity and a few moments at the same time, he ended the kiss and pulled back a little. Her eyes were still closed, and after a moment, she opened them slowly.

"I know you," she whispered. "You are my home."

"And you are mine," he whispered back. "And I have waited too long to find you."

Hannah nodded, and a tear fell down her pale cheek. Tim lifted his hand to wipe it away, then leaned in to kiss her again.

After a few minutes, it was Hannah who pulled away first. "This all feels so surreal, yet I feel more alive now than I have ever felt in this human incarnation."

"I know what you mean. I feel like something has shifted inside."

Hannah looked down at the crystal still nestled in her hands, and she held it out to him. He shook his head. "It's for you. You need it to remain connected to your siblings."

Hannah smiled and put it in her pocket. "Thank you. I have felt a little disconnected from them in recent years. But right now, I feel as though they are merely a whisper away."

Tim's stomach rumbled loudly then, breaking the magic of the moment. Hannah giggled and he blushed a little.

"Shall we go and get some food?" Hannah suggested. "I bet everyone is dying to know what's happening with us."

"I bet they are," Tim said dryly. He got to his feet and then held his hand out to Hannah. When they were both standing, Hannah had to tilt her head up to look at him; he was quite a bit taller than she was. He bent his head down slightly, and kissed her again. He wrapped his arms around her, pulling her in closer, and she responded by wrapping her arms around his neck and kissing him back.

After several more minutes, Tim's stomach growled again, more insistently this time. They broke apart, laughing, and without another word, Tim took her hand and they made their way out of the tent. They walked hand in hand up the path to the house, and when they entered the door, they were greeted with cheers and applause. They both looked at each other and blushed, and were ushered to a table in the corner that had been laid with a vase of flowers in the centre and a lit candle.

They sat down and were served by Violet and Greg, before being left alone to eat. The others seemed to be deliberately engaging in loud conversation, in order to give them privacy.

"Do you think this happens often?" Hannah asked.

"What? Twin Flames meeting each other at the Twin Flame Retreat? I don't know, we'll have to ask. If it happens often you would think they'd mention that in the sales copy."

Hannah giggled. "Yes it is quite the selling point, but I guess they cannot guarantee it happening, and would hate to disappoint people."

"True." Tim reached across the table and put his hand over hers. "Are you sure we aren't dreaming right now?"

Hannah smiled. She turned her hand around and pinched his palm. He pulled his hand away in pain and she giggled. "Nope, we're definitely awake."

Tim shook his head and rubbed his palm. "Guess I asked for that, didn't I?"

Hannah nodded and tucked into her food that was going cold. Tim realised then that the room seemed to be very quiet. He looked over to where the others sat and they all looked away suddenly, like they had all been watching and listening to them. He blushed and concentrated on eating his own food, and the noise level in the room resumed normal levels again. Throughout the meal, he couldn't stop himself from staring at the woman sat across from him. She was truly stunning. How had he not recognised her the moment they'd met? He'd felt attracted to her over the last couple of days, but he hadn't quite

- 68 -

realised the depth of his attraction.

Once everyone had finished eating, they had an hour free to do as they pleased before the afternoon session. Tim smiled at Hannah.

"Would you like to go for a walk in the woods?"

She nodded and they left the house, slipping on their shoes as they went. Walking down the path, hand in hand, Tim's heart was so full, he thought it might burst.

# Chapter Nine

"As soon as everyone is here, we will begin."

Amy looked up from her conversation with Rachael at Greg, then looked around the workshop room. Only Tim and Hannah were missing. She smiled. She'd seen them go off for a walk in the woods, it didn't surprise her that they were late getting back.

"Probably up to no good," Rachael whispered.

Amy laughed and nodded. "Maybe we should go and check the pods, they've probably just got carried away."

"Eww, do you think they're at it?" Mary asked, joining in the conversation.

Greg chuckled and Mary blushed. "The connection when you first meet your Flame is very intense. It can be a little overwhelming."

"Have any other people met their Flames here at the retreat before?" Beatrice asked.

"I think it's happened once or twice before, though it happens most often in the few weeks or months afterwards. We still get letters of thanks addressed to Esmeralda and Mike, for their part in reuniting the Flames."

"And this is where Greg and I came together after a period of separation," Violet chimed in.

Beatrice frowned. "You separated? Why?"

Violet smiled. "That is exactly what this session is about. It's about the different stages you may find yourself going

- 71 -

through with your Flame, how to cope with each one, and how to remain true to yourself and your mission throughout." She looked at Greg who smiled back.

"It wasn't part of the original retreat, this is something that Greg and I have put together based on our own experiences, and I hope that it will help Flames to build a stronger foundation, and a stronger and longer lasting relationship."

Amy nodded in agreement. If they could help other Flames avoid the pain they had suffered, she knew it was a good idea. She frowned when she thought she heard a noise.

"Can anyone hear that?"

Everyone stopped talking, and in the silence, they heard a distant yelling. Without even knowing why, Amy was on her feet and moving to the door that led outside to the balcony, and Greg was just behind her. She opened the door to see Tim running up the driveway. He spotted them and tried to speak, but was winded from the run.

"Something's wrong," Amy said, her senses screaming. Greg was already heading for the stairs, and she was right behind him, Violet and Rachael followed, Mary and Beatrice and Joy seemed frozen in place, looking confused.

Amy ran outside to Tim with Greg. He had just about caught his breath when they reached him, and Amy saw that his face and hands were muddy, and mixed in with the mud was blood.

"Where's Hannah?" Greg asked urgently. "What's happened?"

"The caves," Tim gasped. "We were in the caves, we didn't go too far, Hannah was in front, then, the ceiling, the ceiling," he gasped and a sob rose up, and his tears mixed with the mud on his face.

Greg had already left his side and was running to his shed. Amy reached out to Tim and pulled him into her embrace, while Violet ran into the house to get her phone.

Amy held the sobbing man while Greg came back, riding a quad bike loaded up with ropes, a couple of shovels, a hard hat, and a bagful of equipment. Violet reappeared, on the phone to the cave rescue volunteers.

"I don't know which cave it is exactly," she said loudly over the noise of the quad bike. "My partner is heading that way now, I will give him this phone, so when you get near, call him. Please send an ambulance in case she's badly hurt."

Violet hung up and handed the phone to Greg. Amy could see the fear on her face.

Tim pulled away from her and seemed to be a little calmer. "When the ceiling collapsed, I called out to her, but there was no response. I tried to dig through the mud and the rocks, but it was too much, I couldn't get through." He started crying again, and Amy looked up to see the others standing at the door.

"Tim, let's go inside, Greg is going to check it out, and wait for the rescue team, there's nothing you can do right now."

Tim shook his head. "I have to go back down, I didn't want to leave her there, but I knew I needed to get help."

Violet took his arm. "Let's at least get you cleaned up and put some warmer clothes on, and we'll go back down together."

Amy could tell from Violet's tone of voice that she was afraid Hannah was no longer alive. But Greg looked determined.

"I'm heading down. I'll see what I can do while the rescue team arrive."

"I have climbing experience," Beatrice said, pulling on a jacket and putting on a pair of walking boots. "I'll come with you."

Greg nodded and she climbed onto the quad bike behind him, wrapping her arms around his middle.

"Be careful," Violet called after them as she guided Tim indoors. Greg looked back and nodded, before rumbling down the driveway.

Amy followed Violet and the others back inside, and

realised she was shaking. She started praying to the Angels as hard as she could, that Hannah was still alive, and that she would be okay.

*      *      *

Beatrice held on tight as Greg sped down the rocky, muddy track to the caves. Her heart was pounding and she was worried what they might find. When they reached the fence with Danger signs on it, Greg stopped and switched the engine off. They climbed off the bike, and gathered up the gear, then climbed over the fence, making their way down the steep bank to the groups of caves beyond.

Beatrice didn't know anything about the history of the area, so she had no idea how the caves had been created. She was curious, but she didn't think that now was the time to ask for a history lesson.

When they reached the mouth where the cave-in was, Beatrice's heart plummeted to her feet. It looked pretty solid. She assumed Greg would start shovelling, but was surprised when he turned away and started to head back the way they'd come.

"There's another entrance to this cave," he said over his shoulder, hiking back up the hill. "It's not a very big entrance, but I should be able to get through still."

Beatrice hurried after him, glad that she had been doing so much training recently. Even so, her legs were on fire when they climbed back up the hill to the other entrance to the cave. When they reached it, Beatrice looked at the tiny opening doubtfully.

Greg rigged up a rope around a tree and around himself, strapped his hard hat on, and instructed Beatrice on what she needed to do. He handed her a walkie-talkie and they tested them. Then he started climbing backwards down into the hole.

"Be careful," Beatrice said, echoing Violet's earlier words. "The whole cave could be unstable."

"I know, but I have to try." A few seconds later, Greg disappeared and moments later, Beatrice's walkie-talkie came to life.

"I'm inside, seems fairly stable so far. I'm going along the tunnel, I'll let you know when I've made contact."

"Okay, I'll keep an eye out for the rescue team."

After a few minutes, there was a crackling noise on the walkie-talkie, then nothing. After a further five minutes, Beatrice started to get nervous.

"Greg?" she said into the walkie-talkie. "Greg, are you there?" All she heard was static. She knelt down at the tiny entrance and stuck her head in, to see if she could hear anything. She wanted to call out but didn't want to distract Greg if he was busy trying to find Hannah. Violet's phone vibrated in her pocket, and she pulled it out to answer it.

"Hi, Violet, yes we've found the cave and Greg has gone in through another entrance. He's in there now, but I don't know if he's found her or not, because the walkie-talkies don't seem to be working underground. You'll be here in a few minutes? Okay, I'll keep trying to-" Beatrice broke off at the sound of rocks falling inside the cave. Her heart hammering, she managed to say goodbye to Violet and hang up without making the Old Soul even more nervous about the fact that her Flame was in the middle of a dangerous rescue mission.

"Greg?" she called into the entrance. She heard a few more rocks crashing down, and she forced herself to breathe and calm down. Suddenly, her walkie-talkie crackled to life.

"I've found her. She's unconscious, but breathing, and partially covered in rubble. I'm going to go back and carry on uncovering her, the walkie-talkie doesn't work further in. Send the rescue team straight in, I don't want to move her because she may have spinal injuries."

"I've just spoken to Violet, they will be here in a few minutes." Beatrice heard voices then, and saw Violet, Tim and the rescue team approaching along the path. She updated them on the situation, and told the volunteers to go straight in, because the walkie-talkies didn't work. She got out of their way while they coordinated sending the men in with a stretcher to get Hannah out.

Beatrice went over to Violet and Tim, who both looked equally ashen and scared. She reached out to hold Tim's hand and he looked at her gratefully. They waited for what seemed like hours, but eventually, the rescuers emerged from the tiny entrance with Hannah on a stretcher. Tim stepped forward, but stayed out of the way of the paramedics, who'd arrived on the scene minutes earlier, and immediately began to assess and treat her.

Violet went over to where Greg was climbing out and Beatrice watched them embrace. Greg looked over to where Hannah lay, still and unresponsive.

Beatrice supported Tim as he leaned against her, and soon, the team were ready to move Hannah. They carried her down the path to where the ambulance was parked, waiting. They loaded her up and Tim asked if he could go with them.

"We'll contact her next of kin, Tim, and we'll get sorted and head over there to be with you, okay?" Violet called out. Tim nodded and they closed the doors. The ambulance set off carefully down the track, leaving the three over them stood there in the late afternoon sunshine.

Beatrice turned to Violet and Greg. "Do you think she's going to be okay?" she asked softly.

"It's all my fault," Greg said. "I told Tim about the caves, I should have warned him that they might be unstable."

Violet shook her head. "You couldn't possibly have known. We've explored the caves many times with no problems."

"But what if she doesn't make it?" Greg whispered, a tear making its way down his dusty face. Violet reached up to wipe it away.

"She will. She will make it."

Beatrice looked back to where the ambulance had disappeared. "I do hope so," she said.

- 76 -

# Chapter Ten

"What do you think is happening?" Mary asked Rachael. "They've been gone for ages."

Rachael patted Mary's arm reassuringly and set a cup of tea in front of her. "They'll just be taking their time to get Hannah out of there safely. It's not the kind of thing you can rush."

"Poor Tim, he was just beside himself," Joy said, tears in her eyes. "Can you even imagine anything more tragic than meeting your Flame only to lose her within hours?" She shuddered.

"It's like when Violet met Greg, he saved her from the water, but she had a badly broken leg. Maybe we will only meet our Flames in really dramatic circumstances," Amy suggested.

Rachael smiled. "I'm sure there are Flames who have met in much calmer ways. But I suppose it does test how you feel about someone."

"True, you can see from Tim's distress that he loves Hannah," Joy agreed. She looked up then, as they all heard the front door open. Beatrice entered the lounge first, and Mary jumped up.

"Is she okay? What's happening?"

Beatrice explained what happened, and Rachael went to get the kettle on while Amy got a blanket and wrapped it around her. Shivering, Beatrice accepted the blanket and sat on the sofa. Violet came in and explained that she and Greg would be going to the hospital.

"Would you like us to leave?" Mary asked. She figured the last thing they needed to deal with was guests.

Violet shook her head. "No, there's no need to go early. I'm sure Amy will be able to sort out food for this evening, it's mostly prepared anyway, and then you're welcome to watch a movie or whatever. We'll be back later, and we'll still stick to tomorrow's schedule as much as we can."

Amy nodded. "Of course I can sort it out, just go and be with Hannah and Tim."

Violet smiled gratefully. "Thank you. I'm just going to go change and call Hannah's next of kin, then we'll get going."

Violet left the lounge and Rachael brought in a mug of tea for Beatrice. She accepted it and wrapped her shaking hands around it.

"Well, I didn't envision this weekend being quite so dramatic," Rachael commented.

"It's certainly not what Violet and Greg had planned," Amy said. "Perhaps we could have a small prayer circle, and light a candle for Hannah? We could call upon the Angels to help her heal quickly."

"That sounds like a beautiful idea," Joy said. "Shall we go up to the workshop room? Perhaps we could watch something after, I feel the need to escape into a movie for a while."

The others agreed, and by the time Violet and Greg were leaving for the hospital, they had settled onto the cushions upstairs in a circle, and were beginning their prayer.

Mary settled down and held hands with her fellow Earth Angels, and prayed for Hannah to be healed and whole and well again.

\*　　\*　　\*

Tim sat on the hard plastic chair, a rough blanket wrapped around him, his heart pounding a million miles an hour. It seemed like the journey to the hospital had lasted for hours. And throughout it all, there had been no response from Hannah at all.

They were worried that she may have severe head or back injuries, due to the nature of the accident, but they couldn't be certain until they got her to the hospital to do tests.

As soon as they'd arrived, a team were waiting for them, and Hannah was immediately whisked away. He was doing his best to try and control his thoughts, but he couldn't stop the fear creeping in.

What if she didn't make it? It had been his suggestion to go down to the caves. She had trusted him, even perhaps started to fall in love with him, and now she was fighting for her life.

He held his head in his hands, and tried to remain strong and calm. He imagined her opening her eyes, seeing he was there, and forgiving him.

"Tim."

Tim looked up to see Violet and Greg. Violet sat down and wrapped her arm around him, squeezing him tight, Greg sat on his other side.

"Have they said anything yet?" Violet asked softly.

Tim shook his head. "Nothing."

"I'm sure they're doing everything possible," Greg said, sounding like he was trying to convince himself.

But no words could comfort Tim in that moment. All he wanted was to see Hannah's smile again.

"I called Hannah's next of kin. It was actually a friend of hers, a lady called Sarah. She said she would come straight away, she should be here in a few hours."

Tim nodded. He wondered why Hannah hadn't listed her family as next of kin. Did she not have any close relatives? He didn't even know. They barely knew each other, barely knew anything about each other, and here he was, madly in love with her and praying she would survive.

"I've been where you are," Greg whispered. "You're not

alone."

Tim nodded gratefully. "Thank you."

"Are you Hannah's relatives?"

They all looked up then as a doctor approached them. Tim jumped up. "I'm her boyfriend," he said, not even caring that they hadn't even got as far as defining their relationship.

"And we're her friends," Violet added, getting to her feet too.

"Hannah is stable now, but early tests are showing spinal damage, and head trauma. At this stage it's difficult to tell just how severe the injuries are, but you need to prepare yourself for the possibility that she may either be paralysed, brain damaged or both. We will have to wait until she wakes up to find out."

Tim's knees buckled then, and he felt Greg's arms catch him before he hit the ground. He was led back to the chair which he collapsed into.

"I'm sorry," the doctor said. "I know it's a shock. To be honest, it's a miracle she's alive, considering the circumstances."

"Thank you, Doctor," Violet said, tears streaming down her face. "Can we see her?"

"Yes, I can take you to her, she's in the ICU."

It took Tim a couple of attempts to stand, but managed it with Greg's help. They walked together through the hospital to Hannah's bedside.

Tim's heart broke when he saw her covered in bandages and tubes. He sat on the chair next to her, and carefully took her hand in his.

"Hannah," he said. "Can you hear me?" He heard Violet and Greg sit behind him, but his gaze was fixed upon his Flame. "Hannah," he whispered, determined to reach her. "I love you."

# Chapter Eleven

"My dear Indigo, welcome home."

Hannah blinked and smiled at the figure emerging from the mists. "Gold!" She ran forward and hugged him, and realised then that she was really very small in comparison. She looked up at him and giggled, then she became aware of a second presence. She turned to her sibling and hugged her too.

"Oh my sweet sister! How I have missed you," she said into her ear.

"I have missed you too," her sister replied. "Though I am sad to see you again at the same time."

Hannah frowned and the events of the previous few hours came back to her. "Oh no! I'm dead, I've left Earth." She looked up at Gold. "For good?"

Gold knelt down to her level and shook his head. "It is your decision, dear Indigo, not mine. You have not been human before, so you have not been through this process. But it is at this point that you are asked the ultimate question." He looked at her sister.

"Do you want to stay?" she asked Hannah softly.

"I have just met my Flame," Hannah said sadly. "I wasn't sure that I ever would, that he even existed for me, and we had just met. I wasn't ready to leave him so soon, we barely know each other."

"You can go back," Gold said. "But you may have severe injuries. Your body has been through something quite

- 81 -

traumatic."

Hannah thought it over for a few moments. Though the idea of being in a disabled body scared her, as she had never in her existence experienced having any physical limitations, she really didn't want to leave Tim just yet. She wanted to love him, and experience his love in return. And besides, she didn't need to go back to her planet, because whenever she was in his embrace, she would be home.

"I want to go back."

Gold nodded. "Very well. I wish you the best, dear Indigo. You have a tough journey ahead, and I applaud your strength."

Hannah nodded and turned to her sister. "I love you," she said. They hugged again.

"I will ask the others to send you healing via the Indigo web."

Hannah nodded and pulled away. "Thank you. What do I do now?" she asked Gold.

He pointed to the mists she had emerged from. "You just return. You will wake up in a couple of days."

"Thank you." Hannah turned away from them and headed back to where she had come from.

\*　　\*　　\*

"Do you think Violet and Greg came back last night?" Mary asked Beatrice when they awoke in the pod on the Monday morning.

"I don't know. I guess it depends on what happened with Hannah. I do hope that she made it. I can't even begin to imagine how Tim will feel if she doesn't."

A tear trickled down Mary's cheek and hit her pillow. She had found it difficult to fall asleep, knowing that Hannah was in such a bad condition. She had prayed over and over again until she'd finally drifted off. But her dreams kept waking her up. She felt a little bad that not all of her prayers had been for Hannah. Some of them had been for herself. She prayed that she wouldn't have to go through such an ordeal when she met her own Flame.

"Shall we head inside for breakfast? If we're the first in, we could make food for everyone else, give Violet and Greg a break?"

"Sounds great," Mary replied, wiping her eyes with her hand. She pulled the covers back and got up. They both quickly got dressed and were soon leaving the pod. Mary noticed that the campervan was back, which meant that Violet and Greg must have come home during the night.

They entered the house, and took their shoes off. They went to the kitchen where they could hear the kettle boiling.

"Greg!" Mary went over to him and instinctively hugged him. Since the night they had gone for a walk to see the stars, she had felt close to him, like he was her big brother. "How is Hannah?"

Greg hugged her back, then sighed. "She's not looking so good. She's in a coma at the moment, and even if she wakes up, they think she could either be paralysed or brain damaged, or both."

Beatrice gasped, and her hand flew to her mouth. Mary felt tears welling up in her eyes again. "No, that's awful."

Greg nodded and got three cups out to make tea for them. Beatrice stepped forward and ushered him away to sit down, and took over the tea making. He sat heavily on the bar stool, his weariness evident on his face.

Mary sat next to him and Beatrice set cups in front of them.

"Is Violet still there?" Mary asked.

Greg nodded. "She wanted to support Tim and wait for Hannah's next of kin to arrive. I said I'd come back and make sure that everyone was okay."

"Amy took good care of us," Beatrice said. "We held a prayer circle for Hannah, had food, and then watched a movie."

"That's good," Greg said. "She's been amazing, helping

us out this weekend."

"Have you had any sleep?" Beatrice asked as Greg's eyes closed for a few seconds.

He shook his head. "No, and as tired as I am, I don't think I'd be able to right now. My mind is just too chaotic."

"In that case, go upstairs, do some vibroacoustic work on yourself, and then get a couple of hours sleep. Mary and I are going to get breakfast for everyone else, and if Violet calls we will wake you up."

Greg looked from Beatrice to Mary, and knew he was outnumbered. He nodded slowly, then got up and took his tea with him. "Thank you."

The two women listened to his footsteps slowly climbing the stairs, then turned to each other. "Brain damaged and paralysed!" Mary said. "I just can't even get my head around that. Not when just twenty-four hours ago she was perfectly healthy."

"I know," Beatrice said softly. "Life can change so quickly, the only thing that I find comforting, though it's sad, is that she at least got to meet her Flame before it happened."

"But not for long. The universe should have given them longer together before taking her life in this way."

"Oh, Mary," Beatrice said, putting her hand on the incarnated Faerie's arm. "She's still with us, she hasn't gone home."

"I know, but if she's that badly disabled, what kind of life will she have?"

*   *   *

Beatrice didn't answer. She had wondered the same thing. She couldn't imagine not being able to walk, or to run, or to take care of herself. To be trapped inside a body that no longer worked? She shuddered. Perhaps it would be better to go home than to be in that position.

She got up and started to prepare breakfast for everyone,

and Mary pitched in, setting the tables in the front room and getting everything ready for when the others appeared.

The eggs were boiled and toast was popping up when Rachael and Joy came through the front door, and Amy came down the stairs.

Beatrice and Mary updated them on the situation, and they all sat down to eat, discussing ways they could be of help to Hannah and Tim.

"She's going to need a supportive group of friends around her to help her through this, and Tim is going to need that too. Where do they both live, does anyone know?"

Everyone shook their heads. Beatrice frowned. "Well, no matter where they live, I will visit them as much as I can, and help with exercise and rehabilitation, if that is an option."

"Let's pray it's an option," Joy said.

Beatrice heard footsteps on the stairs and she looked up to see Greg coming down. She got up and pulled a chair out at the table for him. "I'll get you some breakfast, would you like a coffee?"

He nodded gratefully and took the chair offered.

"We thought you might sleep a little longer," Mary said.

"Violet text me, I'm going back in to the hospital, they're getting the results of some tests, and she wants me there."

Beatrice went to get his breakfast, and despite the awful situation that Hannah and Tim were in, she felt a little envious of the Twin Flame connection that Violet and Greg shared. To have that kind of supportive presence in her life would be amazing. She didn't think she had ever had anyone in her life who was one hundred percent supportive of her, and cared for her that deeply.

She placed everything on a tray and took it out to the front room. She set it in front of Greg and he smiled at her. "I really appreciate you guys stepping up to help like this, I cannot apologise enough for leaving you all to fend for yourself, but this has been a very unusual and unique situation. I promise that the majority of our retreats are very calm and injury-free."

"Don't worry about it," Beatrice said. "It's not in any way your fault, what has happened. And I cannot speak for the others, but I feel that what I have experienced and learnt this weekend will help me greatly, not just in helping me to find my Flame, but in my life in general."

There were nods and murmurs of agreement around the table, and Greg nodded. "That's good to hear. I hope that you all meet your Flames, and in a much less dramatic fashion. Please all keep in touch."

"We will," Rachael said. "I will probably head off in a few hours. If anyone needs a ride to the bus station, I am more than happy to take people."

Everyone started making arrangements then, and Beatrice noticed that Greg only managed a few bites of his toast and a sip of his coffee before he stood up from the table. He said goodbye, then picked up his jacket and left the house.

Beatrice looked at everyone around the table. "Let's sort the place out for when they return," she said. "Amy, do you know everything that needs doing at the end of a retreat?"

Amy shook her head. "There's no need, honestly, I can take care of most of it. You guys should make the most of the time to relax and enjoy the woods before leaving. Why don't we all go for a nice walk down to the river? I know the way. I promise to keep us away from the caves."

Beatrice nodded. "Okay, but I will help to clean up a bit before we leave." The others nodded in agreement with her. She started clearing away the breakfast dishes, and with all of them helping, they got everything tidied up quite quickly.

"Everyone want to meet out front in ten minutes?" Amy asked, as she headed upstairs to put some warmer clothes on. Everyone agreed and headed back to their pods.

Beatrice was already dressed warmly enough for a walk, so she spent a bit of extra time just straightening up the kitchen and lounge, wanting it to look good for when they got home. She picked up Violet's copy of The Earth Angel Training Academy from the bookshelf and smiled. She flicked through to a part where Velvet and Beryl are talking, and wondered if Violet was right, that they had worked together in their past life at the Academy. She set the book down, and as she did, a slip of paper fell out. It looked like a handwritten note, and it had Greg's name written on the outside of it.

She bit her lip and wondered if she should read it, after all, it was clearly a private note. But she couldn't stop herself. She opened it to find three lines written in the centre.

*I believed our love to be like the stars shining above, infinite, radiant, everlasting, shining brightly in the darkness, never fading away; but I guess it was just a shooting star after all.*

Beatrice frowned. She wondered if it had been written during the time Violet and Greg had broken up. Sensing that there was a story behind the words, she folded the paper and tucked it back into the book, and made a mental note to herself to ask Violet about it at a later date.

# Chapter Twelve

"Hannah."

"Starlight!"

"My sweet Indigo, I am so very sorry that you are in this situation."

Hannah frowned and focussed on their surroundings. All she could see was white mist. "Am I still dead? What's going on?"

Starlight shook her head. "No, you are alive, but you are in a coma. I have met you here, so that I could warn you of what is to come."

"Like you did in the meditation? Before I opened the box, you warned me that my life would never be the same. I thought you meant because I would be with my Flame, and it would change things. Not that I would be in an accident and end up disabled. Did you know all this would happen?"

Starlight nodded. "I knew your destiny, yes. But it could have been changed. If you had not opened the box, you may not have realised that Tim was your Flame, and you may not have been in the cave accident."

Hannah sighed. "And you didn't think it was a good idea to tell me all of that before because…?"

"Because I shouldn't have interfered at all. But I just couldn't bear to see my friend go through such pain."

"Well, this is the path I have chosen. I could have left and gone home, to my golden city. I met Gold and my sister on the

- 89 -

Other Side. They said I could stay if I wanted. But I chose to come back."

Starlight smiled. "How is Gold?"

"He is good, he seemed the same as ever."

"That's good to hear."

Hannah looked around, as if she expected something to happen or someone to join them. "What now then?"

Starlight took a deep breath. "Now it's time to wake up. It will be difficult for you, but I promise I will be with you every step of the way, and I will do whatever I can to help with your healing."

Hannah nodded. "Thank you." She took a deep breath. "Let's do this."

Starlight held out her hand, and Hannah took it. Starlight's wings unfolded from behind her, and she took flight, taking Hannah with her.

\*     \*     \*

"Tim. Wake up, Tim."

Tim's eyes flew open at the sound of his name and he sat upright suddenly to see Violet peering at him. She smiled. "Hannah's awake."

He looked over to the bed, and saw that Hannah's eyes were open, and that her friend Sarah was sat next to her, talking to her.

He immediately went to her bedside and took her hand. "Hannah," he whispered. "Hannah, I love you."

Her eyes widened slightly, and she tried to smile, but the tubes that were helping her breathe were restricting her movement.

"I'll go get a nurse," Violet said quietly, leaving the room.

"I'm so sorry, Hannah. It was my fault, I shouldn't have taken you in there, I'm so, so sorry." Tears started running down his face, and Hannah shook her head slightly.

He leaned over to kiss her on the forehead, so relieved that she was awake and seemed to be responding, but he was terrified now, what the tests would show.

He looked up as the door opened and Violet returned with a nurse and a doctor. They moved away from the bed while the nurse removed some of the tubes and then the doctor stepped forward to do some basic tests.

"Good Morning, Hannah, my name is Doctor Onan, and I'm just going to do a few tests, to see how things are working. You seem to have suffered from some head and back injuries."

Tim watched helplessly while the doctor worked, and prayed that she would respond to the tests more positively than they had predicted. When the doctor finished, he turned to them and sighed. "I will need to do further tests to be sure, we will have to take her for some scans, I will arrange for that to happen in the next half an hour."

Tim nodded and the doctor left. He resumed his place by Hannah's bedside, and took her hand. "Hey," he said. "Can you, can you feel this?" He squeezed her hand and she nodded a little. His heart skipped a beat. He reached out to touch her legs through the blanket and sheets. "Can you feel that?"

Hannah's eyes met his, and she didn't need to shake her head to know that she couldn't.

"Let's wait until they do the tests," Sarah said softly. "Let's not jump to conclusions too quickly."

Tim nodded and tried to smile at Hannah to reassure her, but he couldn't help more tears from falling.

Forty minutes later, they took Hannah away for more tests, and the three of them went to the canteen to get some breakfast.

Violet sent a message to Greg, to let him know what was happening. "He's going to come back in soon," she said, when her phone beeped with his reply.

Tim nodded. "I hope he got some rest after everything he did yesterday."

"I don't think he got much," Violet said with a shrug. "He was blaming himself for the incident."

Tim frowned. "How could he blame himself? He was the one who rescued her, I was useless."

"Oh, Tim, you weren't useless. And he feels to blame because he told you about the caves, but didn't warn you that they could be unstable."

"He couldn't possibly have known what was going to happen," Tim protested.

"I know," Violet said. "I said the same thing."

They were quiet for a while, and Tim picked at the cereal he'd bought. He wasn't really hungry, but Violet had made him get something to eat.

"Hannah is strong," Sarah said confidently. "Whatever happens, she will get through this."

Violet smiled at her. "How do you know Hannah? I was surprised that she didn't list any family as her next of kin, have you let them know?"

Sarah shook her head. "Hannah hasn't got any close family. But I feel very much responsible for her, like she's my own child."

"Have you known her long?" Tim asked.

Sarah shook her head. "No, we met less than two years ago. She was very helpful and kind to me, and we have been close ever since. She is the godmother to my daughter, Star."

"That's a beautiful name," Violet said.

Sarah smiled. "Yes, it seemed to suit her." She looked like she was going to say something further, but she stopped herself. Tim looked at his watch.

"They might be done now, I'm going to head back to wait."

Violet looked in dismay at his unfinished cereal, but nodded. "We'll meet you back there?"

Tim nodded and stood up. He took his dishes to the counter then headed back to Hannah's room. When he got there, they were just wheeling her back in. He went straight to her bedside, and noticed that her cheeks were wet. He wiped them gently with a tissue from the bedside table.

"Hey," he said. "What happened? Are you in pain?"

Hannah shook her head slightly, but didn't speak.

"Tim?"

Tim looked up to see the doctor in the doorway, who beckoned him out to the hallway. He squeezed Hannah's hand. "I'll be right back."

He left the room, and the doctor ushered him into his office.

They both sat down and Dr Onan sighed. "There's no easy way to tell you this, but I'm afraid that the early tests show that Hannah has fairly severe spinal injuries, that have left her without feeling or function below the waist."

Tim closed his eyes and shook his head.

"But that's not all I'm afraid. It seems that she has also suffered some damage to the brain, which has impaired her ability to speak. Though her hearing and cognition still seem to be intact."

Tim's eyes snapped open and he stared at the doctor. "So you're saying that she can hear me and understand me, but she can't speak?"

The doctor nodded.

"Is it permanent?" Tim asked.

The doctor shrugged. "It's hard to tell at this stage. We will focus on her recovery first, then start working on rehabilitation, and we will just hope that she is able to recover her ability to speak, but you need to prepare yourself for the fact that it may be permanent."

It was just too much. Tim dropped his head into his hands and sat there for a while, his brain just couldn't comprehend what the doctor was trying to tell him.

"I'm sorry I haven't got better news," Dr Onan said. "But the best thing you can do right now, is to be with her."

Tim finally lifted his head up, and nodded. "Thank you."

He left the office, and on his way back to Hannah's room, he saw Violet, Greg and Sarah coming up the hallway.

He told them the results of the tests, and Violet started

crying. Greg held her tight, and kissed her on the head.

"I don't know if I should tell her or not," Tim said. "Though I think she already knows most of it."

"She knows," Sarah said softly. "But like I said, she's tough. With our help, she'll get through it."

Tim nodded. He went into the room, and took his place at Hannah's side. She looked up at him, and his heart ached at the thought that he might never again hear her beautiful voice say his name.

\*     \*     \*

After a nice walk down to the river and back, Amy said goodbye to all of her new friends, as they all set off back to their lives. She had promised to keep them all updated on Hannah's situation, and they had all exchanged details, determined to keep in touch with one another.

She had just made herself a cup of tea when she heard the approach of a vehicle up the driveway. She got up and went to the front door in time to see Violet and Greg getting out of the van.

"Hey," Violet called out tiredly. "Has everyone left?"

Amy nodded. "Yes, they left about an hour or so ago."

Violet came up to her and they embraced. "I was hoping I might be able to see them and to apologise to them."

"There's no need to apologise for anything, they were all fine."

Violet released Amy and smiled. "Thank you for taking over here." She shook her head. "It's been a horrible twenty-four hours." They all headed into the house, and Amy put the kettle back on to make them a drink. When she came back into the lounge, Violet and Greg were sat on the sofa, and Violet was nearly asleep, snuggled into Greg's side.

Amy set the drinks down and sat opposite. "How was she?" she asked quietly.

Greg shook his head, looking like he had aged ten years

overnight. "Not so good. She woke up out of the coma this morning, but they did the tests, and it looks like she's paralysed from the waist down, and the head injury has impaired her ability to speak."

Amy gasped. "She can't speak?"

"No. It seems like she can hear and understand, but she can't communicate."

"That's awful," Amy whispered. "Poor Tim must be beside himself. What is he going to do?"

"I don't know. I mean, it's a lot to take on when you have literally only just met someone, but," Greg looked down at Violet, who was now fast asleep at his side. "I know how he feels. He's in love with her. And if Violet had been in the same condition after her accident in the sea, I would hope that I would have stuck by her too. I love her more than anything."

Amy didn't mention their breakup. She knew it wasn't her place to say anything, or the right time to mention it. But at that moment she thought of it, Greg looked up at her and nodded slightly.

"I know," he said. "It may be difficult to believe that I wouldn't leave her, considering our history, but really, that was only because I wanted the best for her."

Amy smiled. "I know that. I know that you never intended to harm her. But, well, you weren't there afterwards. You didn't see what she was like."

Greg closed his eyes, and Amy regretted saying anything. She was sure that he didn't need to be made to feel bad, he already looked like he had the weight of the world on his shoulders.

"It's in the past now, perhaps we should leave it there."

Greg looked at Amy gratefully. "Thank you." He looked down at Violet again. "I think Violet needs to get some rest, I'm going to take her upstairs. I think I might crash too. I'm sorry we haven't sorted anything out for dinner."

Amy waved her hand. "Don't even worry, I can sort myself out, as long as it's okay for me to stay of course."

- 95 -

"Absolutely. Please don't go before Violet is properly awake again. I think she'll need some Angel support. She wants to visit Hannah again tomorrow too."

"I might go with her."

Greg nodded and got up carefully, trying not to disturb Violet too much. He leaned down and wrapped his arms around her, and though sleepy, she reached up and held onto him.

Amy watched him carry her out the room and up the stairs, and she sighed. Despite the drama and trauma of the previous twenty-four hours, she couldn't help but wish she had the love and support of her own Twin Flame in that moment.

But the likelihood of him just suddenly appearing at the door was slim. So until the moment they met, she would just have to take care of herself. With that thought, she got up and went to the kitchen to find herself something to eat.

# Chapter Thirteen

Beatrice couldn't believe her eyes when she first read the email. Harry purred at her feet, but she took no notice. She hadn't heard from Violet since the retreat, several months before, but she was thrilled to hear Violet's news.

The Old Soul had been asked to do a talk and workshop on Twin Flames in a large venue in London, with the view to tour the country doing talks and selling her books.

Beatrice immediately picked up the phone and dialled Violet's number.

"Hello, Twin Flame Retreat."

"Violet!" Beatrice said. "I just got your email, congratulations!"

Violet laughed. "I know, I still don't quite believe it myself, I was going to call you, but I'm still in shock to be honest."

"It's an incredible offer, are you going to take it?"

Violet sighed. "I've been thinking of nothing else since they got in touch. Thing is, I think we did an amazing job of getting the book done and out there. But I am aware of my limitations, and I could do with the publicity for the book. It would be great if it increased the sales." She sighed. "And to be perfectly honest, we need the money. The last eight months has been pretty tough, and the deal they're offering would mean that we wouldn't have to struggle so much anymore."

"Then what are you waiting for?" Beatrice asked. "Go for

it!"

"It just means that I will have to travel a lot, and Greg will have to run the retreat by himself, which I'm sure that he can do, but…"

"But what?"

"I find it hard to be away from Greg," Violet whispered. "And if the first one goes well, they want me to go on tour with several other authors over the course of a few months."

"I'm sure you'll be able to keep in touch and come home every now and then. Is there perhaps someone who could give Greg a hand with the retreats if he needs it?"

"Amy has offered to help out if I go away, and I know that she would be great at it."

"Violet, you have to go for this."

"I know, I would be stupid not to, wouldn't I? Thank you."

"You're welcome. Have you heard from Tim recently?" Beatrice didn't mean to change the subject so suddenly, but the words were out of her mouth before she could think them through.

"Yes, I spoke to him just a few days ago. Hannah is doing well, she's able to get about in a wheelchair, and she's getting good at sign language, so she's able to communicate a little easier."

"I can't imagine what it would be like, to be trapped inside my own body."

"Me either, it's made me realise just how incredibly lucky I am. I mean, I have Greg, and we're both fit and healthy and able, I'm thankful every day for that."

"Yes, I love going for a run and doing my workouts. Hannah's accident has made me appreciate that all the more."

"Anything happening on the relationship front?" Violet asked.

"No," Beatrice said. "But I'm okay with that. Because it just feels good to no longer feel afraid of being alone anymore. If I am meant to meet him, then I will."

"It's a good way to look at it. You're not afraid of there

being some dramatic incident if you were to meet him, are you? Because I'd hate to think that we'd put you off completely after the retreat weekend."

Beatrice laughed. "No, it's okay, I'm not worried about that. I know that was an unusual circumstance."

"Good. Well, I better go, we have guests arriving soon, and I need to get my head out of the clouds and back into work mode. It was great to hear from you."

"It was great to speak to you too. Send my love to Greg too."

"I will."

Beatrice said goodbye and hung up, then stared at her computer screen blankly for a few minutes before shaking her head and snapping back into work mode herself.

After a few hours of editing, she felt so stiff from sitting still, that she decided to go for an afternoon run to loosen up. She didn't normally go in the afternoon, she preferred to run first thing in the morning, but something was propelling her to get changed and put her trainers on.

Once she got into her stride, her tense shoulders and back started to loosen up, and she relaxed into the run.

She ended up taking a slightly different route to her usual morning run, and enjoyed the different scenery as she veered through a park. She was halfway across the field when she was aware of something rushing at her out of the corner of her eye. She turned just in time to see a large dog running toward her. At first, she began to slow down, but when she saw the look on its face, she started to run faster. She wasn't afraid of dogs, but this one did not look friendly.

She could hear someone calling out frantically, and when she looked back, she could see the dog was gaining on her. Her lungs were about to burst, and she desperately needed to stop, but didn't think it would be a good idea. She looked back round and only registered the tree root a nanosecond before she tripped over it and went flying. She rolled over quickly and sat up, but before she could get to her feet, the dog leapt onto her and she screamed. She tried to push it away from her, but it was snarling and snapping at her face.

Suddenly, the weight of the dog lifted off her and she took her arms from her face to see a tall man wrestle the dog to the ground. Another man came running up then, holding a lead and out of breath.

"Oh my god, are you okay? I never let him off his lead normally, I'm so sorry." Beatrice watched in shock as he went over to the dog who looked up at him adoringly and docilely allowed himself to be clipped back onto his lead. The tall man stood up, released the dog and towered over the man.

"If I ever see you in this park with that dog again I will call the police. If you can't control it, you shouldn't have it. Do you understand me?"

The dog owner nodded quickly, and the tall man stepped around him to offer his hand to Beatrice. She accepted it and he pulled her to her feet. "Thank you," she said, her voice shaking from the adrenalin.

"Do you want to report him to the police?" he asked her.

She shook her head. "No, I'm fine, really."

The tall man turned back to the dog owner, who was inching away from them both. "I will report you if you ever return." He turned back to Beatrice while the dog owner scarpered.

"Can I walk you home?"

Beatrice nodded and realised she was shivering.

"Here," he put his arm around her, and despite the fact that he was a complete stranger, the warmth of his body heat was comforting.

"My name is Ben," he said. "I'm really glad I was there just now."

"Beatrice. And I'm really glad too. Thank you, for saving me."

Ben smiled. "Anytime."

\*       \*       \*

Tim switched the kettle on and leaned heavily against the counter. He had never been so tired in his whole life. The previous few months had been the most challenging times he had ever experienced, and he knew that it wasn't going to change anytime soon.

He made his tea and then took it into the lounge and sat on the sofa. He was having one of his rare breaks, Hannah's friend, Sarah, had taken her out for the day, giving Tim some much needed down-time.

He looked around the room, which still didn't really feel like home, despite the fact that he and Hannah had been living there for four months now. He had sold his business, rented out his flat, rented out Hannah's flat and they had then chosen their new home together, which could be adapted for her wheelchair and for the care she needed. But they'd been so busy, that it still lacked the small touches that would make it into a home. Tim decided he would resolve that, as soon as he had some energy to spare.

He heard the post being shoved through the letterbox and hit the floor, and he got up to see what there was. He was waiting for a letter from his solicitor, and was hoping it would be there.

He picked up the pile, which included some redirected mail from his flat. When he saw the postcard from Nepal, his heart thudded. He turned it over, knowing that he would see Aria's scrawl on the back.

Aria and Linen were travelling again. They had been to Nepal and Thailand and were heading to Bali. Despite the fact that Tim loved Hannah with everything he had, and that he hadn't even thought about Aria once since he had met his Flame, he felt a twinge of envy that Linen had a beautiful, energetic Faerie to go travelling the world with, and he was stuck here, in this place, having to be a full-time carer.

Almost as soon as he felt the twinge, he quashed it. It didn't matter where they were, or what they could or couldn't do, there was no way that he would give up the connection he had with Hannah. She might not be able to speak the words, but she showed him in every way she could how much she loved him.

They had gone through some really tough times, where Hannah had felt like a burden to him, and had tried to push him away, tried to make him leave, but he had stood his ground. He wasn't going anywhere.

As all of his thoughts and emotions and fears tumbled around in his mind, Tim suddenly realised that he was crying. He needed help. Without giving it a second thought, he went to get his phone and found the number he needed.

"Hello, Twin Flame Retreat."

"Greg? It's Tim. I need your help."

Greg listened while Tim filled him in on the last few months, but not just the positive highlights that he had told Violet, Tim told Greg everything.

After a few moments, Greg replied. "So when shall I come to visit?"

Tim sighed in relief. "Any time. I'm sorry I can't come to you, but it's difficult to find decent carers for Hannah."

"Don't even worry about it. We have another retreat booked in for next weekend, but everything is pretty much set. I could come over tomorrow, stay the night and then be back in plenty of time."

"Are you sure that's okay?"

"Of course it is, Tim. I'm just glad that you have asked for help. I know that must have taken a lot of courage to do. Violet has your address, so I will get that from her. Just take the rest of today to chill, I will see you tomorrow, around lunchtime?"

"Thank you, Greg. I really appreciate it."

Greg said goodbye and Tim hung up. Even just telling someone about everything had made him feel less overwhelmed and alone. He wandered around the house for a bit, feeling lost, then decided to go for a walk to get some fresh air, before making a meal for when Sarah and Hannah returned.

He was just lighting the candles on the table when he heard the front door opening, he rushed over to help Sarah get Hannah's wheelchair through the door.

"Wow, what smells so good?" Sarah asked.

"I've cooked us all dinner," Tim said, leaning down to kiss Hannah. She kissed him back, a smile on her face.

"I love you," she signed to him quickly.

"I love you too," he replied. "I hope you two have worked up an appetite."

"I'm afraid I have to get going," Sarah said. "Gareth has cooked and apparently Star isn't feeling well, so I need to get back to tuck her in."

"Oh dear, well I hope she feels better," Tim said, giving Sarah a hug. "Thank you for taking Hannah out for a girly day."

"She'll be fine, Gareth's probably given her too much sugar. And no worries, you know we always have a great time."

She crouched down next to Hannah's chair and they stared at each other for a while. Tim had noticed that they tended to do that rather than speak or sign to each other. He really should ask what they were doing, but it always felt like too private a moment to intrude upon.

Once Sarah left, Tim wheeled Hannah up to the table, and set her food in front of her with a flourish. Though her arms were getting stronger, she had lost some of her motor skills in the accident, and so he always made sure that her food was easy to spear with a fork and eat, so that she could be as independent as possible. He knew that she hated being treated like a child.

"So I heard from Greg today," Tim said, sitting down at the table. "He's going to come visit us tomorrow."

"With Violet?" Hannah signed.

"No, I don't think so, but I don't know, maybe. The truth is, I called him to ask for help, I feel like I need to do the releasing emotion process again, and Greg said he would come

- 103 -

over to do that with me."

Hannah put her fork down and frowned. "Are you okay?"

Tim sighed. "I was just feeling a little overwhelmed today." He reached across the table and put his hand over hers. "I'll be fine, I just needed a little male support I think."

"I'm sorry."

"Don't be silly, you have nothing to be sorry for. You're the one who has had the most to deal with and adapt to, and you have done it all with so much more grace and ease than I think I would ever be capable of."

Hannah's eyes filled with tears. "You made it easy for me," she signed. "I couldn't have done it without you."

Tim shook his head. "If it wasn't for me, you wouldn't be in this situation."

Hannah frowned. "You still feel that way? I thought we'd talked about that."

"I know." Tim sighed. "That's why I need Greg's help to let things go. There are still things that haunt me every day." He reached across with his napkin to wipe her tears away. "Don't cry," he whispered. "I am so very thankful that you are here with me, that you survived, but I do feel guilty that you are trapped inside your body, that you have to suffer in this way."

"I'm not trapped," Hannah signed, getting a little annoyed. "I'm talking to you, I can express myself."

"I know, I'm sorry. Maybe we should talk about other things, I really don't want to upset you like this."

Hannah pulled her hand away from his and picked her fork up to eat her meal, and Tim did the same.

After a few moments of silence, Hannah reached across to get his attention. He looked up at her and she held her left hand to his heart, and her hand right to her own.

He nodded. They were connected forever. And always would be.

# Chapter Fourteen

"Hannah! It's so good to see you, you look great."

Hannah smiled at Greg and Violet and she reached up to hug them both. They came in, and Tim pushed her chair into the lounge.

"Have a seat, guys, I'll get the kettle on," Tim said.

They made themselves comfortable and Violet looked around the room. "This place is lovely. And what a great little village too."

Hannah nodded. She knew that Violet and Greg didn't know any sign language, so she didn't bother trying to speak to them. She did want to talk to Violet more, but she would use her computer to do that, as she found that with an oversized keyboard, she was still able to type, although much more slowly than she used to.

"I hope I've remembered all this right," Tim said, coming in with the drinks. He set the cups down, and handed Hannah's to her.

She accepted the cup with a smile and took a sip. She was worried about Tim, and she really hoped that Greg would be able to help him. He had coped with a lot of changes over the last eight months, and considering they had met just a couple of days before the accident, Hannah was amazed that he had stuck it out. But then, considering the depth of their connection, it shouldn't have surprised her really.

Before long, the two men excused themselves, but before

he left, Tim wheeled Hannah over to her computer, knowing that she would want to chat to Violet.

The program she used would speak whatever she typed in, making normal conversation a little easier. She found that she was able to make more sounds now, than she was able to just after the accident. But they were still garbled and unintelligible, which she found embarrassing, so she preferred to sign or use the computer to speak for her.

"It's good to see you again," she typed. A moment later, the voice repeated her words.

"It's really good to see you again too," Violet replied, taking a seat next to her. "I'm sorry it's taken us so long to visit, things just seem to have been so busy, and I haven't stopped to catch my breath."

"I never got a chance to say thank you," Hannah typed. "For bringing me and my Flame together." Hannah looked over at Violet, who had tears shining in her eyes.

"And I never got the chance to apologise properly, for what happened. I feel awful that the two of you had only just met, when you got hurt so badly."

"It wasn't your fault. And I think it has made us stronger. I know Tim is struggling at the moment, but I have no doubt that he loves me deeply. As I love him."

Violet nodded. "Yes, I can see that he does." She looked at a framed photo on the desk of Hannah and Sarah with little Star on Hannah's lap.

"It's funny, but when I met your friend Sarah at the hospital, I could have sworn I'd met her before. But with all what was going on, I never got the chance to ask her about it."

Hannah grinned and typed quickly. "You still don't know who she is?"

Violet shook her head with a frown. "Should I? Is she famous or something?"

Hannah laughed silently, then pointed to her book shelf. Violet followed her finger and when her hand came to rest on her own book, Hannah nodded.

- 106 -

"She's in my book?" Violet asked, taking the book from the shelf. Hannah reached out for it and flicked through the well-read pages until she reached a certain place. Then she handed it back to Violet.

"'An Angel, with wings that sparkled like they were studded with stars, came to me and told me that I would be the one to initiate the changes…'" Violet's voice trailed off and she looked up at Hannah in surprise. "Sarah is the Angel with stars in her wings?"

"Yes, her name is Starlight," Hannah typed. "And she came to Earth over two years ago, straight from the stars. She is the Angel of Destiny."

Violet's eyes were wide. "Starlight," she whispered. "Yes, that name is very familiar. I think I met her, on the Other Side."

Hannah nodded. "She came here to help you. With the Awakening."

"Why hasn't she got in touch with me? Told me all of this herself?"

Hannah smiled. "She wasn't sure you were ready. But I think you are."

Violet was quiet for a moment. "Just like Velvet in the book, I feel at times as though I cannot see the bigger picture. There is more that you aren't telling me, isn't there?"

"I think it best if Starlight tells you. I have invited her over today too, she will be here at any moment."

Violet sat back in the chair. "Wow, okay, I guess I'd better be ready for this then. Would you like a drink?"

Hannah nodded and Violet got up to boil the kettle. Hannah could hear the murmur of the men's voices in Tim's study, and she hoped that the session was going well.

By the time the kettle was boiled, the doorbell went. Hannah turned her chair around in time to see Starlight step through the door Violet had just opened. The two women stared at each other for a long time, and then suddenly, Violet's hand flew to her mouth in realisation.

"I remember," she said. "I remember talking to you,

among the stars."

Starlight nodded, and remained silent. She took Violet's hand and led her to the settee. Hannah pulled her chair up next to them.

"We're sisters," Violet breathed.

Starlight's face lit up with a dazzling smile. "Yes, my sweet Violet, we are."

Violet shook her head. "This is crazy. I mean, I thought that those conversations had been dreams, or maybe memories of past lives, but they were real, weren't they?"

Starlight nodded. "Yes, they were very real."

"But how are you here? In human form?"

Starlight recounted her decision and her journey to Earth, as well as meeting Hannah, then Gareth and having her child. "I felt that I could be of more help to you here, my sister, than I could from my place among the stars."

Hannah watched the two women, and could almost see the energetic bond between them, glowing like a bright liquid gold. She remained out of the conversation, knowing they had much to catch up on.

"What am I supposed to do?" Violet asked. "I feel as though I am not doing enough, to help with the Awakening, to help Flames to find one another, to complete my mission."

"You are doing everything perfectly. Soon, your book and your speaking career will take off, and you will begin to reach more and more Earth Angels who are in need."

"How did you know about the talks I've been asked to do?"

Starlight smiled. "I am the Angel of Destiny, I know everything. Plus, the lady who gave you the offer happens to be a contact of mine. I told her she should check out your book."

Violet's eyes widened. "Wow, thank you." Violet looked up then and suddenly noticed Hannah. "Oh, I'm so sorry! I forgot to pour the tea." She jumped up and went to boil the kettle again, and then brought the hot drinks over to the table.

- 108 -

Starlight turned to Hannah, and she felt a deep burning heat fill her chest, and expand all the way down to her toes, making her feel normal again for a second.

How are you doing?

She nodded slightly in response to Starlight's voice in her head. *I'm good, I'm worried about Tim.*

Starlight looked over to the door of Tim's study, and closed her eyes briefly. When she opened them, she looked back at Hannah and smiled. *No need to worry, he will be just fine.*

"Are you guys speaking telepathically?" Violet asked, making Hannah jump out of the mini trance she was in.

"Yes," Starlight said with a laugh. "Since Hannah's accident, we have found that we can speak to each other in our minds. It seems we connected when she was in the coma, and the link has remained."

"That's incredible," Violet said. "Though considering you are the Angel of Destiny, and Hannah is an Indigo Child, I guess it's completely normal really."

Starlight laughed. "Yes, after all, what is normal anyway?"

\*      \*      \*

"I'm really very proud of you, I hope you realise that."

Mary looked up at her sister and smiled. "Thank you."

"I mean it. Since the retreat, you've completely turned your life around. New job, no drinking, drugs or clubbing. You even got the pixie haircut you've been talking about for years!"

Mary touched her hair a little self-consciously. She was still getting used to her new haircut; she'd had long hair her whole life, and had never had the courage to cut it off before. But after the retreat, she found she had more confidence, and felt like she could make decisions and make things happen. She also didn't feel the need to escape her life anymore.

"I suppose I feel more comfortable in my own skin," Mary said to Celine. "I don't feel the need to be somewhere else, or doing something else, I'm happy to be here, in this moment."

"Amazing," Celine said with a smile. Impulsively, she reached across the dinner table to hug Mary.

"It's all thanks to you," Mary said. "If you hadn't given me your ticket to the retreat, I would probably be on a dance floor right now, taking goodness knows what."

"In that case, it was most definitely worth it. Though I may still have to go on the retreat myself at some point."

"Do it," Mary encouraged. She picked up her fork and resumed eating the meal her sister had made them both. Over the last few months, they had been meeting every Tuesday for dinner, to catch up with each other and have a good chat. Mary looked forward to their weekly dates, though she wished that she was going on actual dates as well. She was happy in her new job and with her new way of life, but she really did want to find someone to share it with.

"Any luck on the Twin Flame hunt?" Celine asked, making Mary wonder if she could read her thoughts.

She chewed her food and shook her head. "No, maybe I should join an online dating site or something, go on some dates. Somehow, I just don't get the feeling that I'm going to meet my Flame sitting in front of the TV every night."

"Internet dating sounds fun, though promise me you'll be careful, you never know who you might be meeting on there."

"Of course," Mary said. "You know me, Ms. Careful."

Celine raised an eyebrow, probably thinking of all the dangerous and crazy situations Mary had got herself into over the years. "Uh huh, sure."

Mary giggled. "Oh, lighten up, Celine. I promise not to be stupid. I just feel like I've spent the last few months waiting for Mr Right to turn up on my doorstep, and it's not very proactive. I feel like I need to actually be visible to the world."

"No, you're right. I'm just being a worrywart. I just don't want you to get hurt that's all."

"I know, and I appreciate that, I do."

"So, do you want to sign up tonight? We could take some pictures of you and set up a profile and then see who's on there."

Mary looked at Celine in shock. "Um, okay, I guess. I haven't got any makeup on or anything."

"I can do you're makeup first. Oh! This will be so much fun."

Mary frowned. "I think we need to put your profile on there too, if you're that excited."

Celine blushed. "I've already joined several sites. But I haven't had the courage to meet up with anyone yet."

"Well I don't think that double dating on a first date is the way to go," Mary said. "But if you need any support then I would be more than happy to be in the vicinity when you meet up with someone, in case you need someone to rescue you."

"Thank you." Celine finished eating her dinner and then stood up. "Shall we get started?"

Mary looked down at her plate, and scooped up her last forkful. "Okay, let's do it."

An hour later, Mary's sides were hurting from giggling so much. "Are these guys actually for real? Do they honestly think that's attractive?"

Celine shook her head. "I know, it amazes me sometimes, what they come out with. I suppose that's why I've been too afraid to meet them in person. I mean, they could be perfectly nice on their profile, but in real life, they could be a total psycho."

"By that reasoning, you should pick one that seems like a total psycho online, because then he's more likely to be perfectly lovely in real life."

"Huh," Celine said. "I hadn't thought of it like that."

"I'm joking, Celine. Please don't pick out a psycho."

"Hey, what if we each pick one for each other, to meet up with? And no silly choices, we would have to choose someone we actually think we'd get on with."

Mary frowned. "This is feeling bizarrely like an episode of 'Date my Mother', but okay, sure, let's try it. Do we get to see the guy's profile before the date, or are we going to do it blind date style?"

"Oooh, let's do it blind date style, that would be way more fun. And let's both meet them on the same night in the same place, so we can keep an eye on each other."

Mary thought about it for a while. It sounded a bit like a recipe for disaster to her, but part of her was also curious as to who her sister would choose for her. Her own past choices hadn't been best, so perhaps it would be a good idea.

"Shall we take it in turns to look then?"

"Well, I'm afraid I'm going to have to get to bed soon, because I'm on an early shift in the morning. So why don't we just choose for each other later. And if neither of us log into our own profile until after the date, we won't accidentally see the profiles."

"It feels a bit sneaky, messaging guys pretending to be you."

Celine giggled. "It'll be fun. I think I would actually be more relaxed, pretending to be you, I get a bit tense when looking for myself."

"Okay, well, I'd better get going." Mary got up and stretched, and then went about gathering her things. "Thank you for dinner, and for the laugh. It's been fun."

"Thank you for joining me," Celine said, giving her a hug. "Shall we say eight o'clock on Friday night for the date?"

Mary nodded. "I'm sure that can be done. How about meeting at that veggie place that just opened up in town?"

"Perfect." Celine clapped her hands together and squealed. "This is going to be so much fun!"

Mary laughed. "We'll see. Love you, Sis." She opened the front door and stepped out into the cool spring evening air.

"Love you too."

# Chapter Fifteen

Amy picked up the white envelope from the mat and frowned when she recognised her friend's handwriting. She slid her finger under the flap and opened it. When she pulled out the card inside, she nearly fainted in shock.

She ran to her room, grabbed her mobile phone, and called Violet.

"Hello, Twin Flame-"

"You guys are getting married?!"

Violet laughed down the line. "Hey, Amy! You got the invite. That was quick, I only sent them out yesterday."

"Tell me everything! How come this is the first I'm hearing about it?" Amy scanned the card again. "It's only two months away! How long have you been planning this? When did you get engaged? Why haven't you asked me to help?"

"Whoa," Violet said. "One thing at a time. First of all, he only proposed at the last retreat, two weeks ago."

"You've been engaged two weeks and you're getting married in two months? What's the rush? Oh my goodness! Are you pregnant? Am I going to be an aunty?"

"Wow, this is way more questions than I imagined I would get. No, I'm not pregnant, the reason we're getting married quickly is because it's going to be a very small affair which won't take much planning, and because we decided that if I was going to be travelling about, doing talks and workshops on Twin Flames, then we wanted to be seriously committed to

- 113 -

each other first, so that we have that stability and connection."

"I guess that all sounds very sensible, but surely you guys are already committed to each other, why do you need to be married? Will a piece of paper really make much difference?"

Violet sighed. "I guess not, I suppose I would just feel safer, like I have an anchor so I don't become adrift at sea while out there following my mission." Her voice lowered a notch. "To be honest, I told him that we either needed to make a solid commitment to one another, or we needed to set each other free and let go."

Amy's eyes widened. "You gave him an ultimatum? Break up with you or marry you?"

"Sounds awful when you say it like that, but yes. And to be perfectly honest, for a short while, I was afraid he was going to set me free. Because I know that he's never been very keen on the idea of marriage, after what he went through with Carly. But he surprised me on the final day of the retreat, at the farewell gathering, by proposing to me in front of all our guests."

Tears sprang to Amy's eyes. "That's beautiful. Oh my god, did he pick a nice ring? I need to see it. When can I come to visit?"

Violet laughed. "You know you can visit anytime, you don't even need to ask. I will need help with the wedding, if you're up for it. We're just having it here, because we figured that guests could stay over. We're only inviting a few people, I wanted to keep it small, and besides, Greg isn't inviting any family."

"You can count on me. I can come down next week to help with early preparations, and then I can always come down closer to the time. Are you going to decorate and stuff?"

"I guess, I really haven't thought it all through. All I know is that we're going to have an Earth Angel theme."

"Of course," Amy said. "Out of interest, what made you suddenly give him the ultimatum now?"

"We visited Hannah and Tim a few days before the last

- 114 -

retreat. And Hannah had invited her friend Sarah along. It turns out that Sarah and I know each other."

"Yeah, you met at the hospital, right?"

"No, I mean that we know each other from before. In fact, we're kind of related."

"Related? How do you figure that?" Amy moved to the kitchen, and put the kettle on.

"She's my sister. Her real name is Starlight, and she is the Angel of Destiny."

The mug Amy was holding shattered on the tiled kitchen floor, and Amy stared at the jagged pieces at her feet in shock. "Starlight? Starlight is here?"

"You remember her?" Violet asked, a note of surprise in her voice. "Are you okay? What was that noise?"

"I dropped a mug," Amy said, wedging the phone between her shoulder and her ear while she got the dustpan and brush and started clearing up her mess. "I don't consciously remember her, but hearing her name, it was a shock, somehow. Like the significance of her being on Earth is massive."

"It is massive. She said she has come here to help me with the Awakening. And she stressed the importance of the reunion of the Flames, and that in order for more Flames to reunite, and for the world to move into the Golden Age, Greg and I needed to show the world that we were willing to do whatever it took to be together, and to inspire other Flames to do the same."

"Wow. That's a pretty heavy responsibility. Was she suggesting that if your relationship failed the whole world would end?"

Violet laughed nervously. "I hope it's not quite as dire as that, but she did place a lot of significance on our union. And so I guess I felt I had to do something about that. So I gave Greg the options."

"What would you have done if he had chosen to set you free?" Amy asked softly as she emptied the broken pieces into the bin.

- 115 -

"I don't know, I guess I would have had to review everything. I mean, I'm not sure I could have still gone out there and done talks and workshops on Twin Flames when my own Flame had chosen to let me go. But I guess I could have still helped those who aren't with their Flames."

"I'm so glad he took option A," Amy said. "And I'm really glad you have seen sense and are asking for my help with the wedding plans."

Violet laughed. "Yes, well just let me know when you're arriving next week. Right now I have to go, I have a cake in the oven and I don't want it to burn."

"Are you sure you're not pregnant?"

"Bye, Amy, Love you."

Amy smiled. "Bye, Violet. Love you too."

Amy pressed the red button then put the kettle on to boil again. She couldn't believe it. After all the drama, the crazy breakup, and all the stress of the last couple of years, Greg had finally got a clue and realised that he needed to make their relationship more permanent.

She had to admit, she had wondered if he would ever see the light, or whether he'd miss out. For some reason, she got the feeling that there was a time where he had missed out, their relationship hadn't recovered and the world had indeed ended in darkness.

As she poured the hot water onto her teabag, she hoped that it had just been a bad dream.

\* \* \*

"Violet! Congratulations!" Beatrice looked across at Ben who had just brought her the post and he smiled and leaned across to kiss her on the cheek. "I will definitely be there, I just have one question, am I allowed a plus one?"

There was a silence on the line as Violet took in her words. "Are you saying what I think you're saying?" the Old Soul asked.

Beatrice couldn't stop herself from grinning. "Yes I am."

"Oh Angel! That's incredible! I'm so pleased for you. You'll have to tell me all about it."

"I will, I promise."

"Is he there right now?" Violet asked intuitively.

Beatrice giggled as Ben started nibbling at her earlobe. "Yes he is."

"May I speak with him?"

Beatrice frowned. "Um, I guess so, hang on." She held the phone out to Ben. "She wants to speak with you."

Ben took the phone and put it to his ear, and Beatrice pretended to study the wedding invite.

"Hello, Violet," Ben said. He listened for a long while, and then smiled at Beatrice. "Yes, ma'am. I will, I promise."

He handed the phone back to Beatrice, and she took it. "Violet? What was that about?"

"Nothing, Angel. I can't wait to see you both at the wedding. I will make sure there is a pod with your name on it."

"Thank you, I'm looking forward to it too! Let me know if you need any help with preparations."

"I will, thank you. Bye, Angel."

"Bye, Violet."

Beatrice hung up and looked at Ben. "Are you going to tell me what she said?"

"Never," Ben said solemnly, before he closed in and kissed her deeply. As soon as his lips met hers, Beatrice forgot all about Violet and lost herself in his embrace.

When they finally emerged from the bedroom later on, and had showered and dressed, Beatrice sat across from Ben at the dining table and smiled when Harry jumped on her lap and demanded her attention.

"Are you feeling a bit neglected, Harry?" she murmured to her cat. "I'm sorry, baby."

"He actually let me stroke him this morning, I think he may be finally warming up to me."

"That's good, because he has been the number one man in my life for some time now." Beatrice sipped her coffee and watched Ben devouring his toast.

It had been a magical three weeks, during which time they had barely left the bedroom, and Beatrice wanted it to last as long as possible, but there was an annoying voice in her head, urging her to be honest with him about her situation.

Ben stopped eating suddenly and frowned at her. "What's wrong?"

She shook her head, amazed that he could pick up a change in her energy so quickly. "There's something that I haven't mentioned yet, that I think you need to know before we go any further."

Ben set his cup down and leaned toward her, his hand reaching across the table for hers. "What is it?"

Beatrice took a deep breath and let it out slowly. "I'm not able to have children. When I was with my ex, we tried for a few years, and when nothing happened, we got checked out, and they said that the chances of me conceiving were extremely slim. My ex really wanted kids, so he left." Beatrice shrugged. "I've accepted that I'll never be a mother, but I don't want to go through that again. So despite how amazing it's been, and despite our connection, if having children is really important to you, then it would probably be best if you left right now."

Ben's eyebrows raised, but his hand remained on top of hers. "First of all, your ex is an idiot. But if I ever meet him, I will be sure to thank him. Beatrice, I know that we have only really just met, but I'm in love with you. And I would very much like to have a future with you. Whatever that future contains or doesn't contain."

Beatrice blinked rapidly, trying to stop the tears from falling. Neither of them had uttered the L word yet, but she was glad that he just had.

"I love you too," she said. "And that's why I don't want there to be any secrets between us. I want you to know everything about me, and I want to know everything about you."

"I second that motion. And in the interest of honesty and transparency, I am quite happy to have a whole family of cats with you, if having children is not possible."

Beatrice giggled and rubbed Harry behind the ears, who was happily purring on her lap. "That sounds good."

"Well, I don't know about you, but I do need to get some work done today, how about I come back around six-ish and I take you out to dinner?"

"That sounds perfect."

Ben got up and came over to kiss her, and then had to pull himself away. "You're just too irresistible," he whispered. He left the kitchen and appeared moments later with his jacket and shoes on. "I'll see you later," he called from the doorway. Beatrice nodded, smiling to herself. She knew that all he wanted to do was to get back into bed with her.

She got up, gently nudging Harry off her lap and then got herself another cuppa before heading for her desk. She had a pile of editing work that had been growing bigger by the day, and she needed to tackle it before it got too overwhelming.

She switched on the computer and opened the first file, but no matter how much she tried to concentrate on the words, all she could see was Ben's beautiful face.

# Chapter Sixteen

"I wasn't sure you would come."

Mary looked into the eyes of the man sat opposite her, and wondered why she had. "Don't be silly," she said brightly. "I said I would, didn't I?"

Appeased, he continued to eat his meal, and Mary winced at his table manners. After their disastrous double date, Mary had decided not to allow her sister to choose her date for her ever again. But then, she hadn't had much luck with the guys she had met up with since. She wondered if it was even worth the bother. She thought of the email she'd received from Beatrice and sighed. She'd found her Flame while being attacked by a dog, why couldn't that happen to Mary? On some of her dates she had felt like she was being mauled, why hadn't anyone come to her rescue?

Her gaze wandered from her date, who was doing an excellent impression of a pig eating from a trough, and found herself making eye contact with a man sat on a stool at the bar. She smiled automatically, and instead of looking away, he smiled back. Her heart skipped a beat and she felt like he was looking deep into her soul.

Her date had to call her name several times before she tore her gaze away from the stranger and focused on him. "What?" she asked.

"I was asking if you wanted to head to a club after this. Do a little dancing?"

- 121 -

Mary smiled. "No, I don't, but thank you for asking." Suddenly unwilling to waste another second of her time, she dabbed her mouth with her napkin and stood up. "Thank you for the date, but I really don't think this is going to work." She took some cash out of her purse and lay it down on the table. "That should cover my half. Have a lovely evening."

She looked up to see the stranger at the bar watching the scene and she wondered what he was going to do. She looked back at her date whose mouth was hanging open, revealing his half-chewed food. Gross.

She turned and made her way to the exit, but just before she slipped through the door, she felt a hand on her arm, and looked up to see the stranger.

"I'm sorry, I couldn't help but overhear your conversation. May I call you a taxi, or walk you home?"

Mary smiled. "I was planning to walk, I wouldn't say no to some company."

The man smiled and held his hand out. "My name is Rick."

"Mary," she replied, shaking his hand. They stepped outside into the warm, early summer's night and fell into step with each other. Mary snuck a sideways glance at him. He really was very handsome. Much more so than her awful date.

"I guess tonight didn't go to plan, huh?" Rick said.

Mary shook her head. "Not really. I haven't had much luck on the dating front. Apparently it's meant to be a lot of fun, but so far," she sighed. "It's been either deathly dull and boring or just weird."

Rick laughed, and Mary liked the sound of it. "That's not good. Fun is important. What do you like to do for fun?"

"Well, I used to go out clubbing a lot, drink, drugs, that kind of thing, but I got clean and sober a few months ago, so fun has to be found in other ways now." Mary frowned, unsure as to why she had just confessed her past to Rick, somehow, he just seemed really easy to talk to.

"That's really great, that you've changed your life like that."

Mary blushed. "Thank you. It had to happen, I was getting myself into some very crazy and dangerous situations. I went on a retreat that helped me to turn everything around, and to release my addictions."

"So you're into the spiritual stuff then?"

"I guess, in a way. I'm just open to the idea that there is more to life than we think there is."

"I completely agree with you on that one," Rick said. "In fact, do you fancy going somewhere else right now?" He stopped and looked at her, and she was suddenly aware that they were on a poorly-lit street next to the park, and there was no one else in sight. For some reason, a shiver went down Mary's spine and she heard a whisper in her ear.

"Run."

Mary blinked and looked up at Rick, and fear suddenly twisted her gut. Without thinking it through another second, Mary turned away from Rick and took off down the street. She cursed her shoe choice as the high heels slowed her down. Over the sound of her heartbeat, and the clack of her heels, she heard his footsteps gaining behind her.

She pushed herself to move faster, glancing over her shoulder to see how far away he was. Suddenly, she found herself ploughing into something soft and falling over.

"What the hell?" a man with an Irish accent muttered. She looked down to see that she had knocked over a guy and was now laying on top of him in the middle of the street.

"I'm sorry," she gasped. She looked around, but Rick was nowhere to be seen. She scrambled away from her soft landing, and sat on the curb, trying to catch her breath.

"Are you okay?"

She looked up at the man who was offering a hand to pull her up. She took it, and nodded. "I am now, I'm so sorry that I bumped into you. This guy offered to walk me home, but there was something, I don't know, off about him, so I just ran, and he was chasing me. And I wasn't looking where I was going, and-"

"Whoa," the guy said, holding his hands up "Some guy was chasing you?"

Mary nodded. "Yes, he hadn't done anything, I just got a weird feeling about him, and I didn't know what to do." Without warning, Mary realised there were tears streaming down her cheeks.

"Um, are you okay?" The guy shifted awkwardly from foot to foot. "You want to call someone to pick you up?" He held out his phone and Mary shook her head.

"No, it's okay, I'll just go home."

"You're going to walk? What if the creepy guy is still hanging around?"

Mary looked up and down the deserted street and shivered. He had a point.

"Let me just call a cab, then at least I'll know you got back safely."

He dialled a number on his phone, and asked for a cab to the street where they were stood, to wherever she lived. She appreciated that he wasn't asking for her address, how did she know if she could trust him? After all, Rick had seemed like a perfectly lovely guy too.

*And Rick might actually be a nice guy*, a voice in her head argued. *He hadn't actually done anything wrong.* But if he was a nice guy, why did he chase her then disappear when she fell over?

"The cab will be here in a few minutes," the Irish guy said, interrupting her internal dialogue. "I'll wait with you until it arrives, if that's okay."

She nodded. "Thank you. You've been very sweet, this must be a really weird situation to find yourself in on a Friday night."

He shrugged. "I've been in weirder ones."

"Right."

They stood in an awkward silence for a few minutes, until they both heard a car approaching. Mary saw the light on top of the car and she turned to him. "Thank you, for looking after me, I'm sorry I knocked you over."

"Sure, yeah, that's cool."

She got into the car, and told the driver her address. As they drove away, she looked back to see him still stood on the pavement under the streetlight, and for some reason, the idea of leaving him behind made her feel empty. She shook her head and faced forward.

After the craziness of the night's events, she wasn't sure what she felt about anything. Though the idea of removing her profile and staying away from bars for a while definitely seemed like a good idea.

\*       \*       \*

"How about this one?"

Hannah shook her head at Starlight's choice, and continued looking through the clothes rail. They were out shopping for dresses for Violet and Greg's wedding, and Hannah was having fun, even though she was feeling a little bit envious of Violet in that moment.

"Really?" Starlight said. "I think Tim is much more your type than Greg."

Hannah looked up at Starlight, blushing. She'd forgotten that Starlight could pick up on her thoughts and feelings. She sent the thought that Starlight shouldn't be snooping and Starlight grinned.

"Sorry, it wasn't intentional. But I'm serious, you and Tim are amazing together, and that man loves you so much."

"I know," Hannah signed. It wasn't that she wanted Greg, she wanted to be married, and have children.

"Ah," Starlight said, picking up on her thoughts. "I understand that. But you can still have a full and happy life with Tim. Besides, I get the feeling that the advances in technology and science might be able to help you sooner than you think."

Hannah frowned. At her last appointment at the hospital,

- 125 -

it seemed pretty certain that she would never regain the ability to walk or to speak again. But sometimes, Starlight would send her healing, and for a few moments, she would be able to feel her toes, and to make a clearer sound than usual.

So maybe it was possible that one day she would walk down the aisle to Tim, and say I do.

"Anything is possible, my sweet Indigo," Starlight said, holding up the perfect dress for Hannah. "My own Flame taught me that."

Hannah reached out to touch the fabric of the shimmery indigo blue dress and smiled.

"Well, that's you sorted, now I need to find something for me, and something for Star. It was very sweet of Violet to invite us all."

"You're family," Hannah signed. "Of course she invited you. And if it weren't for what you said to her a few weeks ago, there might not be a wedding to go to at all."

"True. I'm so pleased they have decided to make this commitment to each other. She told me they were changing the vows, to fit their union better. Which I think is a great idea. After all, they are creating a whole new paradigm for relationships, it makes sense to create their own terms for their union."

Hannah looked down at the dress on her lap. *Can you see their future?*

Starlight looked at Hannah and smiled. "Yes. Quite clearly."

*What about mine?*

"No need to worry about the future," Starlight said softly. "Just enjoy the present, because presently, I think it's time we bought that beautiful dress and then got something sweet and sugary to eat."

Hannah grinned and nodded. Starlight wheeled her over to the counter to pay, and Hannah thanked the Angels silently for bringing Starlight into her life.

"They're saying 'you're welcome'," Starlight whispered,

as the lady scanned the dress and folded it neatly into a bag.

Hannah paid and took the bag, and the two friends went off in search of sweet treats.

When they got back to Hannah's house later, Tim had already made dinner and laid the table beautifully.

"Are you sure you can't stay?" Tim asked Starlight.

"Sorry, Tim. I would love to, it smells and looks amazing, but I really need to get back to Gareth and Star. Thank you though." She leaned down to kiss Hannah on the cheek. "I had a great time, and I'm glad we found your outfit. Remember what I said, okay?"

Hannah nodded and waved to her friend, then allowed Tim to move her to the table.

"You found an outfit for the wedding?" Tim asked, eyeing up the pile of shopping bags that Starlight had set down at the door.

Hannah nodded. "I'll show you later," she signed.

"I do love a good fashion show," Tim teased.

They ate in silence for a while, and Hannah concentrated on the taste of the food, and the feeling of safety and love that she felt in Tim's presence. Starlight had been right. She needed to focus more on the present moment, and not keep worrying about what might happen in the future. In this moment, she had a beautiful man who cared for her, cooked for her and loved her deeply. She was alive, healthy despite her disabilities, and she had beautiful friends. What more could she ask for?

"Would you like to go to the cinema tonight?" Tim asked. "I know that movie you've been waiting to see has just been released. Thought it might make a nice change to go out. But if you're tired from all the shopping, we can just stream something."

Hannah smiled. "I'd love to go to the cinema with you," she signed.

- 128 -

# Chapter Seventeen

"You look stunning," Amy said, as she finished the final touches to Violet's makeup.

Violet smiled. "Can I see now?"

"Yes."

Violet got up and went to the floor-length mirror propped up in the corner of the room. She bit her recently painted lip and Amy frowned.

"What is it?"

"It just all feels a bit surreal," Violet whispered. She stared at her reflection for a few minutes, then turned to Amy. "Like I'm in a dream."

Amy smiled at her friend, and shook her head. "This is not a dream, it is quite real. And as soon as I have changed into my own dress, and finished my makeup, we are going to go downstairs, out to that marquee and you are going to marry your Flame."

Violet took a deep breath and nodded. "Yes, you're right."

"Knock, knock."

They looked up to see Leona poke her head around the door.

"Leona!" Violet cried, rushing to the door. Leona came into the room, a huge grin on her face. She hugged the Old Soul, careful not to crease her dress.

"Violet, you look amazing."

"I'm so glad you made it! Have you literally just arrived?

- 129 -

Where's Reece, is she here?"

"Yes, only just got here, and Reece is outside with the others, all impatiently awaiting your entrance."

Amy grabbed the clock from the bedside table. "Oh crap, we are late. Don't worry, I will be ready in a few moments." She shimmied into her purple dress and smoothed out the wrinkles over her hips. She tucked a few stray hairs back into her up do, and then applied some more lip stain and some eye shadow.

Then she turned to Violet and Leona and smiled. "Let's not make that poor man wait any longer."

Violet suddenly went a little pale, and Amy reached out for her arm. "What is it?"

Violet shook her head. "Just felt a little dizzy for a moment. I'm okay."

Amy frowned. "Are you absolutely certain you're not pregnant?"

"Oh don't be silly. It's just nerves," Violet said. She picked up her bouquet and took a deep breath. "I'm ready."

The three women made their way carefully downstairs. Violet was sensibly wearing flat ballet slippers, but Amy had opted for heels. She was beginning to regret her choice already.

They reached the kitchen door, which led out to the patio, and Amy could see the marquee in the garden beyond. She was so glad that Violet had given her free reign on the decorations. It looked magical, even if she did say so herself.

They reached the entrance to the marquee, and the harpist took her cue to begin playing. Violet's eyes widened when she recognised the song. It was her and Greg's song, the one that had brought them together again. She took her father's arm, who was waiting for her, and then set off down the very short aisle to her Flame.

Amy walked behind her, and could see Greg's face as they approached. He looked like a blind man seeing a rose for the very first time. His gaze never left Violet's.

Amy took her place beside her friend at the front, and glanced around the small crowd gathered to witness this miracle.

She smiled at Hannah and Tim, and then the officiant began the short ceremony.

"You have all gathered here, on this day, to witness the union of these two souls, as they begin a new journey together. To honour their beliefs, Violet and Greg have written their own vows, and wish to state them now. Violet?"

Violet turned to Greg. "From the moment we met, I knew you. And I knew that I would love you unconditionally, for eternity. So I vow to do just that. To love you in good times and in bad, to see the best in you, every day, to hold you when you need me to, and to allow you your freedom and space when you need to fly. I promise to support you, and help you to succeed in your mission in this life, and to co-create a sacred space and life with you."

Amy's eyes welled up with tears at her friends' words, and though she couldn't see her face, she could tell from her tone that Violet was getting emotional too.

"You are my Twin Flame, my true love, and every moment spent with you will be a moment in which I am truly blessed."

Greg took a deep breath, and appeared to be holding back tears too.

"And you, Greg?" the officiant prompted.

"I dreamt of you, before I saw your face for the first time, and when I saw you in real life, I knew that our fates were entwined. There have been times when I have not been fully awake, and I have not made life easy, but I have loved you throughout every moment. And I promise to love you in every moment from now on. I will support you in your missions, and always be your home."

Velvet nodded, and they turned to the officiant.

"These rings are symbols of the promises made today, and of the eternal bond that Violet and Greg share."

- 131 -

He held out the rings, and Greg took Violet's first, and slipped it onto her finger. Then Violet took Greg's ring and did the same. The two rings had a single rune engraved on them, to match the wooden pendants they both wore every day.

"I now pronounce you, in front of all these beautiful souls on this glorious summer's day, husband and wife."

Greg and Violet grinned at each other, then without needing any prompting, Greg pulled her into his arms and they kissed deeply and slowly, as the audience erupted into cheers and applause.

Amy giggled, and cheered with the others. The kiss went on for a little longer than was probably appropriate for a wedding, but Greg finally released his bride, and they turned and walked down the aisle, to their song once more.

An hour later, after a photographer friend of theirs was satisfied that he had snapped enough pictures of the happy couple and their family and friends, the food was brought out and everyone started to tuck in to the buffet.

Amy was trying to decide which cheese to try, and just as she reached for the cheese knife, someone beat her to it.

"Oh, sorry, were you going to use that?"

Amy looked up into the brightest blue eyes she had ever seen. She shook her head. "No it's okay, you go ahead."

The man smiled and cut off a piece of brie, and put it on his plate before offering her the knife. "I'm Joe, previous participant of a Twin Flame Retreat and now friend of Greg's. And you are?"

"Amy, Violet's best friend."

"Of course, you are the chief bridesmaid after all," Joe said, waving at her attire. "I heard you had a hand in the decorations and food and everything." He took a bite of his cracker. "Nicely done."

Amy smiled. "I just did my bit to help. Violet and Greg are very special to me."

"They are quite an amazing couple," Joe agreed. He looked over to where they stood, chatting to different people while still holding each other's hands.

"So you attended the retreat?"

"Yes, I was booked in for when Esmeralda and Mike ran it, but obviously, with what happened, my booking was cancelled, so I came a few months later, when Greg and Violet were then running it. It was great, I really let go a lot of my past stuff and feel like I'm ready to be with my Flame."

"Their work is quite powerful. I know they have helped many Flames reunite. In fact, you see Beatrice over there?" She pointed to the Incarnated Angel, dressed in a beautiful lilac summer dress, her hand entwined with Ben's.

"Yes?"

"She was on a retreat here just last year, and eight months later, she met Ben, her Twin Flame. And you see Hannah and Tim? They actually met on that retreat."

Joe's eyes widened when he saw Hannah in her wheelchair. "Is it true that the accident happened on that retreat too? But that they still stayed together anyway?"

Amy sighed. "Yes, it's true. They're such a strong couple though. Despite everything."

"That's quite heavy. I mean, kudos to him for taking on that kind of responsibility."

"They're Flames, he loves her. It's not about responsibility."

Joe smiled. "What about you then? Have you met your Flame yet?"

Amy shook her head. "Not that I know of. You?"

"No, me neither. But I know she's out there."

"Can I ask what was in your box?" Amy asked.

Joe laughed. "To anyone who hasn't done the retreat, I have to say, that would sound like a pretty dodgy question."

Amy giggled. "I guess it would."

"In my box was a pair of golden angel wings."

Amy frowned as the description of Athena, who she was in her last life, from Violet's book came to mind. "Did that mean anything to you?" she asked softly, setting her plate

- 133 -

down on the table, suddenly losing her appetite.

Joe shook his head. "No, not really. Though I have always believed in Angels." He tilted his head to one side. "What was in yours?"

"A name," Amy said. "Nick."

Joe's eyes widened and he also set his plate down. Suddenly it felt like everyone around them ceased to exist as he uttered "Nicholas is my middle name. And when I was a kid, everyone called me Nick."

Amy blinked and moved closer to him. When they made contact for the first time, her heart sped up and her breathing became shallow. She stared up at him, and saw for the first time, the whole universe contained within his bright blue eyes.

"Nick?" she whispered. Not caring that they were surrounded by wedding guests, and that less than five minutes before, they had been complete strangers, Amy tilted her head and closed her eyes as her lips met his.

She didn't care what anyone thought. She was finally home.

\*     \*     \*

"Congratulations, Greg," Tim said, shaking his friend's hand. "Beautiful wedding, beautiful bride."

Greg smiled. "Thank you, it all went smoothly, which is good."

"Expecting there to be drama?" Tim asked.

Greg laughed. "No, but, well, you can never be quite sure."

"Is that Amy kissing Joe?"

Both men turned to Violet then followed her gaze to the buffet table. Greg raised an eyebrow. "I didn't even know they knew each other."

"They certainly seem to know each other now," Tim commented.

As the two of them broke apart, and continued to stare at

each other, Violet let out a gasp. "Can you see it?" she whispered.

Tim frowned, he wasn't sure what he was looking for. But when he looked at Greg, he was nodding.

"I can see it. Their auras are blending, and becoming brighter."

"They're Flames," Violet said. "I'm certain of it." The three of them watched for a while, then Joe took Amy's hand and led her out of the marquee, out of their line of sight.

Violet turned to Greg and kissed him. "I'm going to go see Hannah and Sarah," she said, smiling at Tim. "I'll leave you guys to chat."

"I love you," Greg said. She smiled and walked away.

"Do you think there's something going on here?" Tim asked.

Greg looked at him and frowned. "I'm not sure I'm following you, what do you mean?"

"You don't find it weird that so many people have found their Twin Flames here, at this retreat in these woods? I mean, what are the odds, seriously?"

"You're right, I guess I just hadn't thought about it before. It seemed natural to me, that people were drawn here because they were seeking their Flame, and so the universe helped them to find each other. But I'm guessing that we are probably defying many odds every day."

"And that doesn't scare you?"

"It amazes me," Greg said. "But it doesn't scare me, at least, not anymore. Just being here, with Violet, is a miracle in itself, and it took me a little while to get past my fears, and to see how we could make it all work, but one thing was for certain, I could not lose her again."

"I thought you broke up with her?"

Greg sighed. "Yes, I did, but, it was more complicated than that. Let's just say, I know how truly lucky I am that she took me back."

"I can't imagine my life without Hannah. I know we don't

- 135 -

have a normal relationship in many ways, but the extraordinary parts of our relationship make up for that."

Greg smiled and they watched their Flames for a while as they chatted, and played with little Star, who was running around and giggling.

"Is this a private conversation? Or can anyone join in?"

"Leona!" Greg held out his arms to hug his friend. "I'm so pleased that you could make it. I haven't had a chance to meet Reece properly yet, where is she?"

"She's about somewhere." Leona turned to Tim. "Hi, I'm Leona."

"Tim." He shook the hand she offered. "Nice to meet you, Leona. You and Greg travelled around Europe together?"

Leona laughed. "Yes, he picked me up on the ferry on the way to France, four years ago."

"Has it really been only four years?" Greg said. "Feels like I've known you forever."

"I'm not sure whether to take that as a compliment or not," Leona laughed.

"Hey, you said in your RSVP that you and Reece had some big news to tell us," Greg said suddenly. "What was it?"

Leona held out her left hand and Tim whistled when he saw the ring on her finger.

"Oh Lee," Greg said, engulfing her in another hug. "That's great, congratulations. Have you set a date? Violet will be thrilled for you both."

"Well, now it's legally recognised in Europe and the UK, we're thinking of spring next year. We're not in a massive rush, and we want to give her family in Australia time to save up for tickets to come over if they want to."

"Are her family pleased?"

"Yeah, I think she's just sad that her mum never got to meet me, or to know that she was going to propose."

"I'm sure she does know," Greg said softly. "And I bet she's proud of you both. I know I am."

"Thank you. I'm going to speak to Violet, and then get

- 136 -

some more nibbles. You guys have put on an amazing spread, I can't stop myself from eating the miniature chocolate brownies."

"Yeah those things are lethal, I must have eaten at least five before they even made it out here to the table," Greg said.

Leona smiled at them both then went over to the group where Violet sat.

"So what's next? You guys planning to have a family now?" Tim asked.

"We're not in any hurry. Violet's book sales are picking up, and she's started to do talks and workshops about Twin Flames. I think she'll probably focus on that for a while, and build up her career."

"What about you?"

"I'm happy here. I enjoy doing the retreats, and Amy has been helping out with that, I've also hired someone to help out with the daily tasks here, to make it a bit easier. I think this place will continue to grow, and Violet's reputation will also help with that too."

"Sounds like you have it all figured out."

Greg shrugged. "Not really. I mean, who knows what will happen? All I know is that we just need to go with the flow, and whatever happens along the way, we can deal with it together."

"Greg! What a beautiful day!"

Tim moved to the side as other wedding guests came to claim some of Greg's attention, and he found himself wandering out of the marquee to the bench by the pond. He stared at the water lilies, and suddenly noticed a giant dragonfly zooming about the perimeter of the pond, as though he were protecting his territory, which he probably was.

"There you are."

Tim looked up to see Violet approaching him. "Here I am," he said. "Who's looking for me?"

"Your Flame is in need of your assistance. We need help getting her chair into the house."

Tim got up. "Of course." He walked back to the marquee with Violet, back to his Flame, knowing that there was nowhere else he would rather be.

# Chapter Eighteen

"Today was beautiful, thank you for inviting me to come with you," Ben whispered to Beatrice as they snuggled under the covers in their pod.

"Thank you for coming with me, it was much more fun with you. The ceremony was really lovely, don't you think? I love how they made up their own vows and promises, rather than using the traditional ones."

"Yes, they seem like a great couple. Very awake and switched on."

Beatrice yawned. "I don't feel very Awake right now. I knew I shouldn't have had that glass of champagne."

Ben laughed. "Lightweight. One glass and you're drunk."

Beatrice nudged him playfully. "I am not drunk, just a teensy bit tipsy. It was a wedding, drinking champagne is a requirement."

"I managed to avoid it. Champagne is not my favourite." He kissed her deeply, then pulled back a little. "Although, the taste of champagne on your lips is rather delicious."

Beatrice giggled. "Oh really? All I can taste is the cheese sandwiches you've eaten."

Ben pulled a face, making her giggle more, then he kissed her again, turning her giggles into sighs of happiness.

When Beatrice awoke the next morning, nestled in the arms of her Flame, she revelled in the feeling of peaceful bliss that was enveloping her. Despite being in a relaxed holiday mood, Beatrice felt the need to go for a run, the trees and birds were calling to her. She carefully slipped out of bed, and out of Ben's arms, kissing him gently on the head as she did so. He stirred a little, but didn't wake up. She slipped her trainers on and her old running clothes, and then left the pod. She stretched for a few minutes outside, blinking in the bright morning sunshine that was filtering through the trees.

She set off down the driveway, at a slow pace to begin with, speeding up a little when she reached the forest track and felt more warmed up. Each step cleared her mind a little, soon she felt free and joyful, noticing the birdsong that surrounded her, and appreciating that the sun wasn't too warm yet, to make it uncomfortable. She couldn't quite believe that she had met her Flame, and that they fit together so perfectly. She remembered her runs through the woods when she'd attended the retreat. She had thought back then that she was ready to meet her Flame, but she'd really had no idea just how amazing it would be when it happened.

Details of the previous night flashed through her mind and she smiled. She could definitely get used to a lifetime of nights like that.

She did the loop trail and twenty minutes later, was walking back up the driveway, when she heard shouting and what sounded like someone being hysterical. She frowned and walked faster toward the house, feeling an awful wave of déjà vu wash over her. Was someone hurt again?

When she reached the house, the door swung open and Violet came out, looking dishevelled in an old pair of jeans and a torn jumper. The contrast to her appearance the day before was striking.

"Star has gone missing," Violet said when she saw her, not bothering with a greeting. "Sarah is beside herself. Greg and Tim have already gone down to check the caves, Joe and Amy have headed to the river, and I have called all the neighbours and the police."

Beatrice blinked in shock. "I'll wake Ben, where do you

want us to look? I've just been out running the loop, and I didn't see her."

"Hannah and Starlight are staying here, Leona and Reece said they would just spread out and scour the woods, maybe you and Ben could join them. Gareth is out there somewhere too." Violet shook her head. "We don't know how long she's been gone, she was missing when Sarah and Gareth woke up this morning."

"She's only a toddler, barely walking, she can't have gone far?"

"You wouldn't have thought so." Violet sighed and finished lacing up her boots. "I've got my phone on me, and I have everyone's numbers who are out there. If you find her, then let me know."

"I will." Beatrice watched Violet set off down the path, then she hurried away from the house to the pod she and Ben were sharing. She went in and shook Ben gently. "Ben, wake up, we need to go and look for Star. She's gone missing."

Ben's eyes snapped open as he woke suddenly. "Shit, really?" He threw the covers back and jumped out of bed, pulling on his trousers and shoving his feet into his shoes. "How long has she been missing?"

"Since before Sarah and Gareth woke up this morning. She wasn't in her bed. Everyone is out looking right now," Beatrice said, grabbing her mobile phone and putting it in her pocket. "I said we'd go through the woods, Leona and Reece are doing the same."

Ben nodded and they headed for the door of the pod. They went west of the house, into the trees, and immediately started calling out her name.

"She's so small," Ben said. "She can't have gone far."

"That's what I said."

They walked quickly, avoiding the brambles and tree roots, and after fifteen minutes, Beatrice's voice was getting hoarse from shouting Star's name.

"Wait," Ben said, holding his hand out. "Can you see

that?"

"What is it?" she whispered.

Ben took off through the trees, and Beatrice ran after him. A few yards away, Beatrice saw the pink fabric on the ground, and recognised Star's jacket. Ben dashed forward and scooped the sleeping child up off the ground. She woke up at the movement and looked at Ben, her eyes wide. Beatrice thought she was going to start screaming, but instead she smiled.

Beatrice sighed in relief that she appeared to be okay and unharmed. "Star!" she said, fumbling in her pocket to get her phone. "Your mum is so worried about you! Why did you come out here by yourself?"

Star pointed at the tree she'd been curled up underneath, and Beatrice looked at it, but didn't understand. "Is there something special about this tree?" she asked.

Star nodded. Beatrice found the house number on her phone and pressed the green button. It was answered after half a ring.

"Yes?"

"Sarah, it's me, Beatrice, we've found Star. She's fine. She was asleep under a tree."

"Oh my goodness! Thank you so much!" Sarah dissolved into sobs.

"We're coming back now, I'll call Violet to tell her to call everyone else." Beatrice hung up and called Violet's number, and the three of them started to make their way back. Star twisted around in Ben's arms so she could watch the tree as they walked away.

"Violet, we've got Star, she's fine. We're heading back to the house, we'll see you there," Beatrice said to the voicemail that picked up. She hoped that Violet got some reception soon and got her message.

They reached the house where Sarah was waiting outside for them. She ran up to them and reached for Star, who leapt into her mother's arms. "Don't ever do that to me again!" Sarah said, hugging her tightly.

- 142 -

"She seemed really attached to the tree we found her under," Ben commented. "Like there was something special about it."

Sarah shook her head. "She does love trees. I think she sees and hears more than we can imagine."

"Well she's safe now. Shall we head inside? I'm sure everyone will appreciate hot drinks and some brunch when they get back," Beatrice suggested.

They headed into the house, and as they sorted out the food, gradually the search party all returned, all looking incredibly relieved to see Star was healthy and fine.

"Not quite the way I imagined brunch after the wedding," Violet joked as she joined Beatrice in the kitchen.

"I was thinking that perhaps you guys should put a warning on the whole Twin Flame thing too," Beatrice said as she cracked more eggs into the frying pan.

"What do you mean?"

"Well, it seems that finding your Flame is a dangerous business."

Violet laughed. "True. I'm so glad that you weren't hurt by that dog, that sounded really scary."

Beatrice nodded. "It was scary, must admit, I wasn't particularly fond of dogs before, but I'm even less so now."

"Can I do anything to help?" Ben asked, coming into the kitchen. Beatrice reached up to kiss him and smiled. "We were just talking about you, my hero."

Ben blushed. "I wouldn't go that far."

"You rescued me from that dog, and then you found Star in the woods, I would say those were very heroic things."

Ben accepted the plates of food Beatrice handed him, and took them into the other room.

Violet giggled. "Oh bless, I think you embarrassed him."

"He'll get over it," Beatrice said. "He loves it really. Now then, can you find out who else wants eggs?"

\*       \*       \*

Hannah ate her food and watched her friend as she helped Star to eat her boiled egg. She was so pleased that her goddaughter was safe and sound, but something was puzzling her. She reached out in her mind to Starlight, who then turned to look at her.

Why didn't you just connect to her and bring her back? Or tap into your universal connection and see where she was?

Starlight sighed and shook her head slightly. My fear blocked it completely. I couldn't link to her, or to my own true self. It felt like I was inside a dark box, trapped and unable to do anything.

Hannah nodded. She knew the box that Starlight spoke of. It was a terrifying place. From her own experience there, she knew that all you had to do was to step outside in order to see the solution, or to connect and think clearly again. But when you were in that place, it was almost impossible to see the exit.

*I understand,* she thought to her friend. Starlight nodded and re-focussed on helping Star to eat. Hannah reached out and rested her hand on Starlight's and her friend smiled at her gratefully.

Once everyone was full, they all dispersed to their own spaces, to get changed and ready. Hannah knew that Violet and Greg were planning some activities for the afternoon, for all the wedding guests, before they then headed off on their honeymoon. They were going to La Rochelle, in France, where they had first met.

Tim took Hannah to their pod, which Greg had made wheelchair friendly, just for her. And they got changed and ready. Hannah could sense a heaviness in Tim's energy, but didn't know what it was.

"What's wrong?" she asked him.

He sighed. "Going down to the caves this morning to search for Star just brought back awful memories of last time we were here. It's just made me feel a little down, that's all."

Hannah nodded. She didn't really remember much of the

- 144 -

incident, thankfully, but she knew that Tim still had nightmares about it at times.

"It was brave of you to go down there to look," she signed.

Tim shook his head. "What else could I do? Little Star means a lot to me, and I know she means the world to you. I had to do what I could to find her. I'm just glad she wasn't down there."

"Me, too." Hannah thought for a moment. "Do you wish we could have children?"

Tim shook his head. "You're the only family I need and want," he reassured her. "Besides, Sarah and Gareth will probably have more, we could just borrow theirs if we feel the need."

Hannah smiled. That was true.

They headed out to the garden, where everyone was gathering in the marquee for the activities. Hannah looked around at the group of Earth Angels surrounding her and smiled. Yes, they had all the family they needed right there.

- 146 -

# Chapter Nineteen

"Have an amazing time," Amy said, hugging Violet tight. "Don't worry about this place, I'll be here."

Violet nodded. "Thank you, Angel, for everything. Couldn't have done all of the wedding preparations without you." Violet dug her hand into her pocket and pulled out a small box, then handed it to Amy. "A little something to say thank you."

Amy took the box, and opened it to find two golden wings on a necklace. She smiled, and looked up at Violet. "Thank you."

"Hey," Joe said, coming over to them both. "That's them, that's the golden wings that I found in my box."

Amy and Violet looked at each other and giggled. "In that case, you have found the right one," Violet said to Joe, giving him a quick hug. "Now, look after my favourite Angel, or you'll be hearing from me."

Joe nodded quickly. "Yes, ma'am."

Violet shook her head. "Goodness, being addressed in that way makes me feel old. Anyway, we'd better get going, or we won't get to our B&B until late."

Amy watched her set off down the path to the campervan, and smiled as she thought of the little goodies and gifts she had hidden in the van for them to find.

"So, we'll have the place to ourselves once everyone has gone then?" Joe whispered into her ear.

- 147 -

Amy nodded. "Yes, we will." She looked up at him. "I'm staying here for the two weeks Violet and Greg are away, how long can you stay?"

"I have to be back in work on Wednesday, so I can stay until Tuesday night."

Amy's heart sank a little at the thought of him leaving.

"But I can be back Friday night for the weekend if you want me to be."

Amy grinned and reached up to kiss him. "Now that sounds like a plan."

The afternoon went by in a blur of goodbyes and cleaning, but after the last guest had left, and the place resembled its normal self again, Amy and Joe crashed out on the cushions in the workshop room upstairs and put a movie on.

"Did you have any idea at all, that this was how the weekend would end?" Joe asked, as he ran his hand through Amy's hair repeatedly, lulling her into a meditative state.

"Uh uh," she murmured. "I was so focussed on making the wedding as magical as possible for Greg and Violet, I hadn't even really thought about myself, or what might actually happen."

"It was magical," Joe said. "I've been to a few weddings recently, and there seemed to be so much focus on spending money on pointless things, and on everything being perfect, and yet yesterday was perfect, because the only focus was on how much Violet and Greg truly love each other."

"Which is how it should be," Amy said. "I never understood why people married each other out of convenience, or a sense of duty or out of loneliness. That's not the path to happiness."

"I agree. You do it for true, unconditional love, or you die as a bachelor or a cat lady."

Amy giggled. "Exactly."

They watched the moving image on the projection screen for a while, but neither of them had been paying any attention to the story that was unfolding, or to the drama of the characters.

"Shall we go to bed?" Joe suggested, echoing Amy's thoughts. She picked up the remote and switched off the movie, then accepted his help to get up off the floor cushions.

They went to the guest room, and Amy hesitated when she closed the door behind them. The previous night, they had been very restrained, and had said goodnight after a passionate kiss, and Joe had retired to his pod for the night. But with no one else there, Amy knew that she would feel safer if he stayed with her in the house, but she had never slept with anyone within forty-eight hours of meeting them before, and she was a little afraid.

He came over to her, where she stood frozen by the door and he cupped her face in his hand and smiled. "Let's just sleep. I just want to be next to you."

Amy nodded, delighted yet amazed that he knew exactly how she felt and what she was thinking.

They got ready for bed, and slid underneath the covers, and Amy closed her eyes, and enjoyed the feeling of his body pressed against hers, his heat warming her to the core.

\*   \*   \*

Mary looked through the wedding photos that her friends had posted online, and wished that she had attended the wedding. She'd received her invite, but the idea of going alone just didn't thrill her. She saw pictures of Hannah and Tim, of Beatrice and her Flame, Ben, and even noticed that Amy seemed to be with someone too. Had everyone who had attended the Twin Flame Retreat with her found their Flame already? She hadn't heard anything from Rachael or Joy, but perhaps that was because they were too busy with their new Flames too.

Mary sighed. Perhaps her Flame wasn't out there? She remembered her vision, during the meditation at the retreat, of being in the underwater garden with a Merman. Had that even been real? She realised afterwards, that Violet mentioned an underwater garden in the Earth Angel Training Academy. Perhaps her imagination just took that information from the book and made a really realistic vision from it.

She could still remember the feeling of his calloused hand around hers though, and the sparks as they made contact.

Her imagination wasn't that good, surely?

She stopped looking at the wedding photos and shut her computer down, wishing that she didn't have the day off work. Having too much time to herself to think was not a good thing. Without thinking it through too long, she got up and went to her room. She found an old rucksack, and stuffed an old blanket in it before going to the kitchen to pack random food and drink to make up a picnic of sorts. Then she grabbed her sunglasses and left her flat. She headed to the nearest bus stop, and hopped on the first bus into town. Though she lived just half an hour from the sea, she hardly ever went there, and she decided it was time she spent more time there. Besides, it was August, and she had yet to spend an entire day outside that summer. She was in desperate need of some vitamin D.

She hopped on another bus in town, and when the sea came into view through the windows, she smiled. She had definitely made the right decision. She pressed the button to get off at the next stop, then made her way down to the beach. Once she hit the sand, she walked along until she left the tourist crowds and found a quieter stretch, further away from the town. Then she took out her blanket and laid it on the dry sand, before sitting in the middle of it. For a long time, she just stared at the waves, and lost herself in the sound of them pounding onto the sand. There wasn't much wind, but for some reason, the waves seemed quite fierce.

She could see some surfers, a little further up the coast, also away from the crowds. She envied their courage. She had always been a little afraid of the sea. She liked to watch it, but to get in it, to allow herself to be moved by the currents, scared her. She didn't know why though. She had never had a bad experience that she could remember.

Mary closed her eyes and tilted her head toward the sun, feeling the warmth soaking into her skin. Suddenly, despite her earlier thoughts, she felt the need to feel the water for herself, so she pulled off her shoes, and rolled up her jeans. She looked around to check there was no one nearby who might steal her picnic, and then she got up and walked to the water's edge. She got close enough for the water to cover her toes, and she winced. Considering it was coming to the end of the summer, it was actually still quite cold. She went in a little further, glancing back to make sure her stuff was still there.

When she got ankle deep, and the waves splashing against her legs were starting to soak the bottom of her jeans, she stopped, and closed her eyes.

She listened to the sea, the cry of the lone seagull above, and the pounding of her own heart in her ears. She nearly didn't hear the screaming above all of that, but when she did, her eyes snapped open and she looked around for the source.

She saw someone at the water's edge a few yards away, and the screaming appeared to be coming from them. Without thinking it through, she started splashing her way toward them.

"My baby!"

Mary scanned the water and saw a dark figure in a wetsuit with a small form tucked under his arm, pulling him into to the shore. Another surfer joined him, and together they got the young boy to land.

Mary arrived just as they lay him down and started to perform CPR. She instinctively went to the mother and tried to calm her down as she sobbed hysterically.

"Shh," she said. "Let them do the CPR, they'll get him back. Do you have a phone?"

The woman held out her bag to Mary, who took it and rummaged around for her mobile. She pulled it out and dialled 999, and asked for an ambulance. She didn't like the look of the young boy, his skin looked so blue; she wondered how long ago he had stopped breathing.

"They're on their way," she said to the woman, tucking the phone back in her bag. She put her arm around her, and they watched as the two surfers worked tirelessly on him, trying to get him to breathe. But there was no response. Finally, Mary heard the sirens, and she looked up toward the road and saw the ambulance pull up. She let go of the mother and ran toward them, to let them know where they were.

Her heart was pounding now, she knew from her first-aid training that it was taking too long for the boy to start breathing again, and that every second counted.

The paramedics followed her back to the water's edge, and took over from the surfers. But after a further few minutes, it became apparent that the boy had gone.

When the paramedics stopped, and checked the time of death, the mother collapsed in Mary's arms and started screaming. Tears streamed down Mary's cheeks as she tried to support her. They both sank to the sand and the woman sobbed hysterically into Mary's arms as the paramedics started to get the boy onto a stretcher to take his body away. One of the surfers came over to them, and reached out to the mother.

"I'm so sorry," he said in a familiar Irish accent. "I'm so, so sorry." He looked at Mary, and when their eyes met, a flash of recognition went across his face. "Hi, again," he said.

Mary nodded, and with the paramedics help, she got the mother to the ambulance, to go with him to the hospital. She told the paramedic that the woman's phone was in her bag, so they could call someone to be with her. Then she walked wearily back to where she had left her blanket and rucksack, but when she got closer, she saw that the tide had risen to beyond where she was sitting.

"Oh shit," she muttered. But then, she couldn't get too upset over a few lost belongings. A woman had just lost her son. In comparison, it didn't seem worth worrying about. She wasn't entirely sure she how she was going to get home though, without her purse.

"Looking for this?"

- 152 -

Mary looked up to see the surfer holding her stuff, and she smiled. "Thank you. I was just wondering how I was going to get home without my purse."

The surfer handed her the blanket and rucksack. "I'm just pleased to know that you got home safely before. Afterwards, I wished I had given you my number, so you could have let me know you were safe. Did that guy ever bother you again?"

Mary laid the blanket out and sat down. She shook her head. "I've never seen him since. He completely disappeared." She pulled out some food from her rucksack and patted the blanket next to her. "Would you like to share my picnic?"

He smiled and sat down on the sand. "My wetsuit will soak your blanket," he said, accepting the packet of crisps that she offered him.

As she settled onto the blanket, and her heart calmed down, the drama of the previous fifteen minutes sunk in, and tears started falling again.

"Are you okay?" he asked.

She shook her head. He put the crisps down, moved to her other side, and put his arm around her. She leaned into him, and despite the dampness of his wetsuit, appreciated the gesture of comfort.

"It's happened a few times," he said softly. "Sometimes we manage to save them, sometimes we're not so lucky. Instead of thinking they have died, I like to think they have gone home to the ocean. I know it's where I'll be headed one day."

Mary looked up at him in surprise. "That's kind of beautiful."

He smiled. "I think it's just my coping mechanism. It feels less painful that way. Not that pain is necessarily a bad thing."

"You're pretty deep for a surfer," Mary said.

He laughed. "Thank you. Though I'm not sure that's a compliment to the rest of my friends."

Mary pulled a tissue out of her rucksack and blew her nose. "I don't even know your name."

He held his hand out to her. "I'm Sean, it's nice to meet you again…?"

"Mary," she supplied. "It's nice to meet you too, Sean. Thank you, for providing a soft landing, again."

Sean chuckled. "My pleasure. Though I wish our meetings had been a little less dramatic."

Mary laughed. "Yeah, my life is usually pretty boring. Well, even more so since I stopped dating."

"That guy really put you off, huh?"

She nodded and nibbled on some bread. "It did shake my faith in the opposite sex, I will admit."

"We're not all crazy, you know. Some of us are just decent guys trying to do the right thing."

Mary smiled. "Yes, you are." She passed him a drink, and he took it and gulped it down. She was feeling better now, though she still felt a little shaken by the whole incident. But there was something very calming about Sean's presence.

"So what brings you to the seaside on a Monday?"

"Is that your way of finding out if I am unemployed?" Mary teased.

"Not at all, it's just that usually only surfers, beach bums, single mums and families on holidays frequent these parts in the week, and I was curious."

"Fair enough. I had the day off, I was fed up of my own company, and I'd had enough of looking at a friend's wedding photos from the weekend, so I decided to get out for a few hours."

"That's cool. In case you were wondering, I do work, but I freelance, from home mostly. So when the surf is good, I head out here, and then just work later into the night to make up for it."

Mary shrugged. "I wasn't judging, there's no need to explain."

Sean laughed. "I guess I'm just used to having to explain my crazy lifestyle."

They ate in silence for a while, then Sean sighed. "I'd

better go. I do have a bit of a backlog at the moment, and a meeting at six." He got to his feet. "Thank you for the food, I appreciate it. I hope you enjoy the rest of your day off."

"Wait," Mary said. "What if nothing else dramatic happens and we never meet again?"

Sean smiled. "Then it was not meant to be."

He walked away down the beach, and Mary watched him go, feeling lost suddenly. She wished she had pushed him for his number. But for some reason, as she watched him pick up his abandoned board and head to the car park, she couldn't move.

When his car disappeared down the road, Mary turned back to the sea, and this time, there was no one there to comfort her as the tears fell.

*       *       *

"I love that photo of us," Tim said. "I think I'll get it printed and framed. We need to put some more photos and stuff around the house, it doesn't really feel homey enough yet."

Hannah nodded in agreement as she looked at the photos Tim was scrolling through on his laptop. She stopped him at one point, and it stopped on a photo of her and Starlight.

"Huh, that's mad," Tim said. "Sarah almost looks like she's got wings, the way the light is behind her."

"She is an Angel," Hannah signed. "Could you print that photo for me too?"

"Of course." Tim created a new file of photos he wanted to get printed. He really was keen to make the house more like a home. "Hey, how about we go shopping to get some stuff for the house, I don't know, some art for the walls, cushions, that kind of thing?"

Hannah smiled. "I'd like that."

Later, Tim put the laptop away and began their usual evening routine, which included Hannah's physical therapy exercises.

"You want to sleep in your bed or mine tonight?" he asked. She often slept in a special bed that they'd bought, to alleviate pressure and to stop sores from developing, but sometimes she liked to sleep alongside him, and every night, he would ask her where she wanted to be.

"With you."

He smiled and got her ready for bed, then lifted her out of her chair, into the double bed. He pulled the covers up, and she picked up the book from the bedside table to read while he locked up the house, switched off the lights and got ready for bed himself.

The routine was so natural to him now, that he barely noticed the fact that he had to do everything twice. Once for Hannah, then again for himself. After the overwhelm he had been experiencing a couple of months before, he now found it all very easy to deal with. He didn't know if it was thanks to Greg's treatments or just that he had found his stride, but it all seemed to be a lot easier now. And rather than feeling drained or tired, he found himself looking forward to each day. His love for Hannah was growing daily, and after witnessing Greg and Violet make such a beautiful commitment to each other, he decided that as soon as I could find the perfect iolite engagement ring, he was going to ask Hannah to marry him.

He slid into bed next to her, and she put her book down. He leaned over to kiss her, and she wrapped her arms around him and kissed him back. "I love you," he whispered, smoothing her hair out of her face. She stared into his eyes, and he sensed the sentiment coming from her in return. He wished he could hear her say the words though. He knew she could make sounds, but that she was embarrassed by how garbled they were. He had suggested trying to have speech therapy, to see if she was able to say some words again, but she had refused. She said she preferred to sign or use her computer to speak for her.

"Good night," he said, kissing her once more. She smiled up at him, and he rolled to his side and switched off the lamp.

He turned back to her and she curled up into his side. Within moments, they were asleep.

- 158 -

# Chapter Twenty

Beatrice flipped over the calendar to October, and smiled at the photo of the black cat next to a pumpkin. "This one looks like you, Harry," she told her cat. She loved Halloween. She just couldn't believe it was October. The year seemed to have gone by so fast. It amazed her that she had been with Ben for four months already. It would be their five month anniversary on the twenty-fifth. She circled the date with a red pen to remind herself to do something nice for him, when a thought occurred to her. She flipped back to September, but didn't see her usual mark. She flipped back to August, then to June, and realised that the last time she had marked her period on the calendar had been at the end of June, just before the wedding.

She thought back over the previous two months, she must have just forgotten to mark it surely? Her periods were very regular, she'd not missed one before.

It was a few minutes before she considered the possibility that she might be pregnant. She had lived with the idea of never having children for so long that to even consider it now seemed ridiculous. But was it really that crazy a concept?

Ben was at work, and she was meant to be editing, but instead she found herself getting up, putting shoes and a jacket on and grabbing her handbag before heading out the door. She jumped in the car and headed into town, and halfway there, she was aware of her hands shaking.

"Get a grip, Beatrice. The likelihood is that you're just

- 159 -

going to waste your afternoon and a lot of money on pregnancy tests, and nothing will come of it. Just calm down."

She pulled into the supermarket and dashed in, almost forgetting to lock the car in her haste. In the pharmacy aisles, she picked out several different tests, of different brands, and then went to the self-checkout, so she didn't have to deal with anyone's prying eyes or questions. She got back to the car, and the thought crossed her mind that she should actually pick up cat food and some other essential items, seeing as she was at the supermarket, but she ignored those thoughts and headed straight home so she could pee on several sticks.

She hurried straight to the bathroom, giving Harry the briefest of pats on the head on the way past. Once safely locked in, she pulled open the first packet and as she got the stick out, she realised that she didn't actually need to go. So she went to the kitchen, got a glass and a jug of water, and started drinking as fast as she could.

Ten minutes later, she peed on the first stick.

It was positive.

Two jugs of water and another seven sticks later, Beatrice was certain. She was pregnant. She sat on the bathroom floor in shock. She had never allowed herself to hope, to dream, to imagine this moment. And so she had no idea how to feel. She thought of her ex, who had left her when she found out she was unable to conceive. She could see now, why the universe hadn't let it happen with him, and why it had stopped her from having children until now. Clearly, she was meant to have Ben's child.

She heard the front door open and close, and she snapped out of her daze. Ben was home early. She pulled herself to her feet and gathered up all of the sticks. She knew that she should probably break it to him more gently, especially seeing as he had accepted and was happy with the idea of not having kids; but she was just too excited to be calm.

She burst out of the bathroom, holding all the positive tests, and he froze in the bedroom, in the act of removing his work clothes.

"Beatrice, are you okay?" he asked.

She went over to him and held the tests out to him. He dropped his tie on the bed and took them from her. After he'd looked at the fourth one, realisation dawned on his face. "Are these all positive? Are you pregnant?"

Beatrice nodded, a huge grin on her face. Ben threw his arms around her, and hugged her, then he kissed her hard.

"Are you serious? We're going to have a baby?"

"Yes," Beatrice said, laughing. "We are."

\*       \*       \*

"I'm really glad you're here, Amy," Greg said as they got ready to serve dinner to the retreat participants.

"Well, I know you would prefer it if Violet were here instead of me, but I do love working here." Amy took two plates out to the guests and set them down on the table. They smiled and thanked her and she dashed back to the kitchen for more.

"I do wish Violet were here, but at the same time, I'm really proud of her, and what she is doing. Plus, all of her talks and workshops have increased our customer base. Next year we're going to have to hold even more retreats than usual because of it."

Amy took another two plates that Greg had filled. "Then it will all be worth it. I'm sure the speaking and touring round the country won't be something she does forever. She'll soon be back here with you, running this place and hopefully writing more books. I really want to know what happens next."

Amy left the kitchen as Greg started laughing. "You know what happens next!" he called out.

Amy served the food to the last two guests, then made sure that everyone was happy before going back to the kitchen to eat herself.

"True. But I'd like to know what happens next from

Violet's point of view. I'm sure there is still so much more that she remembers about being at the Academy that she's never told me."

Greg handed Amy her dinner, and then sat at the breakfast counter with her to eat.

"Have you spoken to Violet today?"

Greg shook his head. "Spoke to her last night, she was shattered after an all-day conference. But she said that it was going well, and she's made some really good connections."

"That's good." They ate in silence for a while, just listening to the murmur of conversation and clinking of china and silverware from the other room. Amy could tell that something was bothering Greg, and she knew from spending the last few months with him, that he was unlikely to offer the information freely. So she decided to just ask him outright.

He sighed. "I just wonder sometimes, if it was the right thing to do, getting married, when Violet has so much to do, and so many people to meet. Why would she want to be tied to me, to here?"

Amy shook her head. "Oh Greg, don't you get it? It's only because of that fact that she has you, that she is secure in your love, that she is able to go out into the world and do those things. That tie, that bond to you, is what helps her to help others. If you cut her loose and set her adrift, she wouldn't have achieved nearly as much as she has. She would have got lost."

Greg was quiet for a while, and Amy wondered what he was thinking. She hoped that she had said the right thing; she just couldn't imagine having to help her friend through another breakup from her Flame.

"Just focus on your mission, and support Violet when she needs it. And then that will give her permission to do the same. That way, you will both do what you need and want to, but you have each other's love and support if things get tough at any point."

Greg nodded. "Okay, I guess that does make sense. Thank

you."

Amy smiled. "Any time."

"How are things going with Joe? He's a great guy."

"Amazing. We've been meeting up every chance we get. I've been staying at his quite a lot, as it's a bit trickier him staying with me at my parents," Amy chuckled. "We've been away in the camper a couple of times too."

"I kind of miss the camper days. Seeing Leona again and going to France for our honeymoon brought back so many memories of our travels across Europe. It really was a great experience."

"What was it like being back in La Rochelle?"

"It was great. I really think that it would be good to retire there some day."

"You would leave this place?" Amy was surprised. She didn't think they would leave, considering Esmeralda and Mike had left it to them.

"There was a note in Mike's will, that Violet and I shouldn't feel that we have to stay here, but that if we were to sell, we would need to make sure that it stayed as a retreat of some sort."

"That's reasonable enough. Do you think you'll start any retreats anywhere else?"

Greg laughed. "I guess that would depend on whether we could actually make this place financially viable. Though we are doing much better than when we initially took over. But that's because of the work Violet has been doing."

"I guess if other people wanted to create Twin Flame retreats you could do a franchise kind of idea."

Greg nodded. "Yeah, that could work. We would have to figure out how that would all work."

"Well, you don't have to figure it all out tonight," Amy said, clearing away their empty dishes. "But we do need to work out what movie we're going to play for everyone."

"I think I can just about manage that," Greg said. "I'll go and set it up. Thank you, Amy."

- 163 -

Amy accepted his hug of gratitude, squeezing him tightly. She put their dishes in the dishwasher, then after Greg had ushered everyone upstairs to watch the movie, she cleared away the rest of the dirty dishes and cleaned up the kitchen. Rather than watching the movie, she planned to call Joe to see how his day had gone. She smiled to herself as she thought of him, and she silently thanked the Angels for bringing them together.

\*     \*     \*

"Oh my goodness! Hello! I didn't know you were coming!"

Hannah smiled at Violet, who was hugging Starlight at her side. Violet then leaned down to hug her too; she wrapped her arms around the Old Soul, and breathed in her perfume. It was a familiar and comforting smell.

"Have you guys been here the whole day?"

"Yes," Starlight said. "And we both agree that you were the best one up on that stage."

Violet blushed bright red. "Aww, that's really sweet of you, but there were some incredible people up there with me today. I've made so many notes."

"There's no need to be so humble, you're amazing, just accept it. Now, are you hungry? Because Hannah is starving and I have to say, I am too, and seeing as I am child-free for the day and can actually stay out past dinner time, I think the three of us should go out to celebrate."

Violet nodded. "I am really hungry. I'll just go get my stuff, and I'll meet you outside?"

"Excellent." Starlight wheeled Hannah down the aisle to the lobby of the hotel, and they waited out the front for a few minutes until Violet joined them, her jacket on and bag in hand.

"There's an amazing Italian place just down the road, I've been there a couple of times now, and they treat me like one of the family."

- 164 -

"Perfect," Starlight said, looking at Hannah who agreed.

They made their way there, and Hannah shivered a little. The October air was getting a bit chilly later in the evenings now.

Starlight stopped suddenly, and Hannah heard her rummaging in the rucksack on the back of her chair, and seconds later, she laid a blanket across Hannah's lap and tucked it in. Hannah smiled and signed her appreciation. Having the psychic link that they did was very useful at times.

They entered the Italian and were indeed greeted like long-lost family members. They made sure there was plenty of space for Hannah's chair at the table, and when Starlight told them they were celebrating, they immediately got three champagne glasses out and popped the cork of something bubbly.

The three ladies settled at the table, and then, full glasses in hand, they raised them, and Violet looked over at Starlight with a frown. "What are we celebrating exactly?"

"We are celebrating the fact that you are following your life's mission, that you are Awakening Earth Angels, and taking the world into the Golden Age."

Violet's eyes were as wide as saucers when she finished. "Have you seen it?" she whispered. "Will we experience the Golden Age?"

Starlight smiled at her sister. "If you keep doing what you're doing, we've got a very good chance."

Violet nodded, looking a little overwhelmed but excited at the same time. "I'll drink to that," she said, clinking her glass to Hannah's and Starlight's.

"To the Golden Age," she said.

"The Golden Age," Starlight echoed. Hannah just smiled and then sipped the champagne. She didn't plan to drink too much, because her medication didn't really agree with alcohol, but she figured a little with her meal wouldn't hurt.

They ordered way too much food, and spent the next couple of hours nibbling their way through the feast, while the owners plied them with more wine.

It was a good thing that no one was driving that night, Hannah thought to herself. She blinked then, her eyesight seemed to have gone a little fuzzy around the edges. She heard voices and turned to look, but there was no one there. She concentrated and could almost hear someone calling her name. She closed her eyes, and answered them.

# Chapter Twenty One

"Hello? Sarah? What is it?"

Before she had even begun to explain, Tim was already out the door, car keys in hand. He got in the car and heart pounding, he cut Sarah off. "Where? What hospital? I'm on my way."

He got the name of the hospital then hung up, pulled out of the driveway and hit the road much faster than he should have. He sped down the road, with absolutely no regard for the speed limits. He had heard the words 'unconscious' and 'not responding' and there was nothing else in his mind other than getting to his Flame as soon as possible.

What felt like a lifetime later, but really was only about an hour later, he pulled into the hospital car park and shoved the car into a space. He ignored the ticket machines and sprinted into the building, heading for A&E. When he reached the waiting room, he saw Violet and Sarah and made a beeline for them.

"What's going on?" he asked breathlessly. "Where is she?" He registered the looks on their faces and his heart stopped. "What?" he whispered.

"Oh, Tim," Violet whispered. "I'm so sorry, she went into cardiac arrest on the way here. They tried to resuscitate, but they couldn't get her back."

Tim shook his head. "No, no, that's not possible. It's just not. No, it's not. Where is she? WHERE IS SHE?"

"Sir?"

Tim turned away from Violet and Sarah to see a doctor standing there. "What?"

"I will take you to her, if you'd like," he said softly.

Tim nodded, aware that he was completely losing it, and not caring. He looked back at the women.

"We'll come with you," Sarah whispered.

The three of them followed the doctor down the corridor to a private room, where Hannah lay on a bed, looking like she was asleep. Tim approached her still form, and tears began streaming down his cheeks.

"Hannah?" he whispered. "Hannah, can you hear me?"

He felt Violet and Sarah either side of him, supporting him.

"She's gone, Tim," Sarah whispered. "She's gone home to the Angels."

"No," Tim cried. "No, she wouldn't go without saying goodbye, she wouldn't." He touched his Flame's face, pale and cold, then he lay his head on her chest, and when he heard no heartbeat, he broke down.

"Don't leave me here," he whispered. "Please don't leave me here alone."

But there was no answer. Her spark had been extinguished.

A few hours later, Tim sat in the house, alone with only Hannah's wheelchair and a million framed photographs to remind him that she had existed.

Sarah and Violet had tried to insist on staying with him, but he needed to be on his own. He just couldn't understand how he had gone from having Hannah there one minute, to her being gone the next. He hadn't even had the chance to propose to her, even though he had bought the ring, just two weeks before.

He picked up the frame on the coffee table, and stared at the photo that they had both foreseen in their meditations at the retreat. She had worn the green top often, because she

- 168 -

loved the part it had played in connecting them.

He sighed. She'd had so much more life to live, so much to do, to experience. How could she be gone? It just didn't make sense.

He set the photo down and pulled her favourite blanket off the back of the settee, and wrapped himself in it.

"Hannah?" he whispered to the empty room. "If you can hear me, please do something to show you're here. Anything."

But there was nothing but silence, and the beating of his own heart.

\* \* \*

"I don't understand, Gold, I was happy with my life, why did the Angels call me back?"

Gold knelt down so he was level with Hannah, and sighed. "You were doing magnificently, my Child, but the Angels, and your siblings, felt that your role in the Awakening was too big for you not to be able to communicate more widely. So they decided it would be better for you to come back home, and then return to earth as a walk-in."

"A walk-in? Take over another's body? Like Laguz did?"

"Yes. Exactly."

"But what about Tim? We were in love, and so happy, he won't understand. Will I still get to be with him if I go back?"

"I'm sure that if we find a suitable body then yes, it will be possible. Of course, he may take a little while to get used to the idea, after all, he will be grieving Hannah, in the body that he knew her in."

She shook her head. "This is really confusing. Are you sure it was necessary to do it this way?"

"Yes, it was. Because you see, Tim was doing an amazing job, of caring for you the way he did, but his role beside you in the Awakening needs more from him than as a caretaker. Together, you are going to be instrumental in taking the world into the Golden Age. We need you both in top physical shape."

Hannah sighed. "If you really think it's that important, then I will have to take your word. But what I don't understand is, why didn't Starlight warn me of this? Surely she knew?"

"She didn't know exactly when it would happen, but she had an idea it would happen, yes. She didn't want to upset you, I'm sure." Gold bit his lip. "How is she, is she happy? Well?"

"I don't think she's very happy that her best friend and godmother to her child just died, but other than that, she's very happy."

"Child?" Gold whispered. "She has a child?"

Hannah frowned. "Haven't you been watching? I thought you'd have known?"

Gold shook his head. "I have refrained from doing so, as it was thought to be counter-productive to my work."

Hannah nodded. "I can understand that. So where do I go until a suitable body becomes available?"

"I think the best place will be the Academy, where the Rainbows still reside. I will be able to call you here easily from there. If you go back to your planet, it may take too long."

"Okay, it would be good to spend some time with the Rainbows." She looked up to see her sister approaching from the Angelic Realm. "Sister, it's good to see you again."

They hugged tightly. "So good to see you again too. Are you going to wait at the Academy?"

"Yes, it seems to be the best option. Feel free to visit me, if you have the time to."

"I would like that. See you soon, sister."

"See you," Hannah echoed, before walking away into the mists toward the Earth Angel Training Academy.

\*    \*    \*

Mary watched the casket being lowered into the ground, her vision blurred with the tears flowing freely down her cheeks. She looked around the other Earth Angels, her friends, who were all as inconsolable as she was. It seemed so cruel, for

Hannah to survive the accident, only to lose her life because of a reaction between her medication and alcohol.

The vicar's words were meaningless to her, all Mary could think of was how fragile life was, and how anything could happen at any moment. She thought of the young boy who had lost his life to the ocean, and she thought of Sean.

If she was honest, she had thought of Sean every day since they'd met again on the beach. Everywhere she went, she kept an eye out for him, but their paths had not crossed again.

Was it not meant to be? Or did she just have to try a little harder? She saw the others with their Flames, and saw them supporting each other, needing each other, loving each other unconditionally. And then she looked at Tim, stood there on his own, with no one to love him unconditionally anymore. Tears streamed down her cheeks faster, and she made a resolution to find Sean. Life was too short, and too precious to wait for fate to deliver to her what she wanted. She need to go out there and get it for herself.

The rest of the funeral was just as heart-breaking, though Star was doing her best to cheer everyone up. Mary watched the little girl running around, and knew then that she wanted a family too, she didn't want to be on her own anymore, going to her sister's for dinner because she had no one else to share a meal with.

"Mary, how are you? I'm sorry we haven't been in touch too much since the retreat."

Mary looked up to see Violet standing there, and she pulled out a chair for the Old Soul. "It's okay, my life has been pretty busy since then. I got a new job, and I have stopped drinking."

"And got a great haircut," Violet said with a smile. "I don't think I'd ever be brave enough to have a pixie cut, even though I think it looks amazing." She ran her hand through her nearly waist-length hair and smiled.

"I like long hair on you, it's more old-soulish, somehow. I'm sorry that I didn't come to your wedding, I just felt a bit awkward."

"Don't worry about it, I completely understand. Before I met Greg, I hated weddings, going on my own just made me feel awful."

Mary nodded and sipped her drink. She smiled when Star nearly tripped up onc of the restaurant waiters. "I have met my Flame," she said, without realising that she was going to mention it.

Violet's eyes widened. "You have? When? That's amazing."

"A few months ago. We met when he helped me get away from a dodgy guy, long story," she said, waving her hand dismissively when Violet looked concerned. "But we didn't exchange details. Then we met again, on the beach. He surfs. But then that makes sense, considering he was a Merman in my meditation at the retreat."

"Oh yes, I remember that, you met him in the underwater garden."

"Yes, that's right."

"So, what happened then? Have you been seeing him since?"

"No, we didn't exchange numbers again. And I've kicked myself ever since. I only have his first name, too, so Googling him hasn't yielded much success."

"And you're sure he's your Flame?"

"As sure as I know my own name."

"Then you will meet again, I am certain of it. Was he Irish?"

Mary frowned. "How did you know that?"

"In your box, in one of the meditations, you had a map of Ireland."

Mary's hand flew to her mouth and she gasped. "I'd forgotten all about that! He has an Irish accent, but I haven't asked him where he's from." They were quiet for a moment, and Mary sighed. "I was thinking, earlier, that I shouldn't leave it to fate to bring us together, but that I should go and find him. Do you think that's a good idea?"

Violet smiled. "Yes, I do. Sometimes, fate needs a helping hand. I should know."

"Thank you."

Violet nodded and went to speak with another Earth Angel, leaving Mary alone with her thoughts. She couldn't wait to leave, perhaps if she got on the road now, she could get to the beach before it got too dark.

She made her excuses and said her goodbyes to everyone, giving Tim a longer hug than she normally would, in an attempt to comfort him. Then she went out to the car she'd borrowed from her sister and headed home.

Three hours later, she pulled up into the beach car park. The sun had already set, and darkness was falling fast, but she had to try. She got out and walked toward the sand, and saw that the sea was flat and calm. So the chances of him being there were very slim. She continued to the water's edge anyway, and breathed in the salty air. She stood for a while, watching the light blue sky turn into an inky indigo.

She didn't hear the footsteps on the sand over the sound of the gentle waves.

"I thought you would never come."

She turned around to see Sean, a smile on his face. "What do you mean?" she asked.

"Since the time we met on the beach, and we didn't get each other's numbers, I kicked myself for suggesting we leave it up to fate. I've been here, on this beach, looking for you, every single day since, just in case you came back to find me."

Tears filled Mary's eyes. "I'm sorry," she said, "I'm sorry that it has taken me until now to realise that fate sometimes needs a little help."

"No need to be sorry," Sean said, stepping closer and holding his hand out to her. "You're here now, that's all that matters."

She took his hand and stepped closer. "Yes I am," she replied. She closed the rest of the gap and reached up until her lips met his. As he kissed her deeply, her sadness and loneliness and the whole rest of the world disappeared.

## About the Author

Michelle lives in England, and when not writing and publishing her own books, she helps other Indie Authors with their own publishing adventures. She has known all her life that she wanted to write books. It is more of a calling than simply a passion, and despite her attempts to live in the normal world, she has finally realised that she would much rather live in a world full of magic and mystery.

Please feel free to write a review of this book on **Amazon**, or even just click the *Like* button. Michelle loves to get direct feedback, so if you would like to contact her, please e-mail theamethystangel@hotmail.co.uk or keep up to date by following her blog – **twinflameblog.com**. You can also follow her on Twitter **@themiraclemuse** or 'like' her page on **Facebook.**

To sign up to her mailing list for monthly newsletters, visit:
**michellegordon.co.uk**

## *The Earth Angel Series:*

## The Earth Angel Training Academy *(book 1)*

Velvet is an Old Soul, and the Head of the Earth Angel Training Academy on the Other Side. Her mission is to train and send Angels, Faeries, Merpeople and Starpeople to Earth to Awaken the humans.

The dramatic shift in consciousness on Earth means that the Golden Age is now a possibility. But it will only happen if the Twin Flames are reunited, and the Indigo, Crystal and Rainbow Children come to Earth, to spread their love, light and wisdom.

While dealing with all the many changes, Velvet struggles to see the bigger picture. When she is reunited with her Flame for the first time in many lifetimes, her determination and resolve to fulfil her mission falter...

## The Earth Angel Awakening *(book 2)*

'No matter how overcast the sky, the stars continue to shine. We just have to be patient enough to wait for clouds to lift.'

Twenty-five years after leaving the Earth Angel Training Academy to be born on Earth as a human, Velvet (now known on Earth as Violet) is beginning to Awaken. But when she repeatedly ignores her dreams and intuition, she misses the opportunity to be with her Twin Flame, Laguz. Without the long-awaited reunion with her Twin Flame, can Violet possibly Awaken fully, and help to bring the world into the elusive Golden Age?

## The Other Side (of The Earth Angel Training Academy) *(book 3)*

Mikey is an ordinary boy who just happens to talk to the Faeries at the bottom of his garden. So when an Angel visits him in his dream and tells him he must return to the Earth Angel Training Academy in order to save the world, despite his fears, he understands and accepts the task.

Starlight is the Angel of Destiny. By carefully orchestrating events at the Academy and on Earth, she can make sure that everything works out the way that it should, even though it may not make sense to those around her.

Leon is a Faerie Seer. He arrives at the Academy as a trainee, but through his visions he realises that his role in the Awakening is far more important than he ever imagined.

## The Twin Flame Reunion *(book 4)*

Greg and Violet are among many other Earth Angels who are reuniting with their Twin Flames. They must work through their own fears in order to be together, but at times, it's just too overwhelming.

Aria and Linen left the Other Side hand in hand, to become humans on Earth. Despite being afraid of forgetting everything, Aria's memory remains intact. But when she finds Linen, he has no memory of her at all.

Charlie experiences an Awakening, and meets his Twin Flame. But when he is unable to control his anger, he changes his future forever.

Starlight leaves her Twin Flame on the Other Side, and goes to Earth, so she can assist Violet and the other Earth Angels with the Awakening. But she is not prepared for everything that comes with being human.

Leona has a vision of her Twin Flame, and decides to search for her. But when they find each other, Leona can See that it may not last.

## Visionary Collection:

## Heaven dot com

When Christina goes into hospital for the final time, and knows that she is about to lose her battle with cancer, she asks her boyfriend, James, to help her deliver messages to her family and friends after she has gone.

She also asks him to do something for her, but she dies before he can make it happen, and he finds it difficult to forgive himself.

After her death, her messages are received by her loved ones, and the impact her words have will change their lives forever.

## The Doorway to PAM

Natalie is an ordinary girl who has lost her way. There is nothing particularly special about her or her life. She has no exceptional abilities. She hasn't achieved anything miraculous. Her life has very little meaning to it.

Evelyn is the caretaker at Pam's. The alternate dimension where souls at their lowest point find the answers they need to turn their lives around. The dimension dreamers visit, to help people while they sleep.

One ordinary girl, one extraordinary woman.

One fated meeting that will change lives.

## The Elphite

Ellie's life is just one long, bad case of déjà vu. She has lived her life before - a hundred times before - and she remembers each and every lifetime.

Each time, she has changed things, but has never managed to change the ending.

This time, in this life, she hopes that it will be different. So she makes the biggest change of all - she tries to avoid meeting him.

Her soulmate. The love of her life.

Because maybe if they don't meet, she can finally change her destiny.

But fate has other ideas...

## I'm Here

When Marielle finds out that a guy she had a crush on in school has passed away, the strange occurrences of the previous week begin to make sense. She suspects that he is trying to give her a message from the other side, and so opens up to communicate with him, She has no idea that by doing so, she will be forming a bond so strong, that life as she knows it will forever be changed.

Nathan assumed that when he died, he would move on, and continue his spiritual journey. But instead he finds himself drawn to a girl that he once knew. The more he watches her, and gets to know her, he realises that he was drawn to her for a reason, and that once he knows what that is, he will be able to change his destiny.

*If you enjoyed this book, you might want to try the Visionary Collection, also by Michelle Gordon. Here is the first chapter of The Elphite:*

# Chapter One

He'd only just made it in time.

Breathing heavily, he slumped into the first empty seat he came to and tried to relax. So far his holiday had been one stressful event after another.

First, he'd forgotten his passport and had to speed home to retrieve it. Then, with only minutes to spare before the flight check-in closed, he'd been stung for having too much weight in his suitcase. Not having enough time to deal with it, he'd paid the extra, though now the dent in his wallet meant less spending money when he finally got to Spain. He'd sprinted to the boarding gate, made it onto the plane, and then found himself sitting next to a lady who smelled like she'd spent the last twenty years locked in a house full of cats.

After holding his breath for nearly two hours, the plane had finally touched down, and he'd got to the luggage area, only to find that the airline had lost his suitcase. They said it may turn up, in which case they'd send it to his hotel in a few days, but that meant until then, he had nothing to wear but the clothes on his back.

At least he'd made it onto the train from the airport. Of course, it had cost him an extra thirty-five euros to get the train from the airport in Zaragoza to his hotel in Barcelona. So much for taking it easy and having a break from his normally stressful life. He was beginning to wish he hadn't gone for the last-minute deal and had stayed somewhere closer to home instead. He sighed. At least he was only a few hours away from his destination now.

Breathing a little easier, Luke opened his eyes and sat up straight. He grabbed the rucksack at his feet and started to rummage through it, looking for the thriller that he'd brought with him. A sigh and a movement out of the corner of his eye made him look up.

The girl sat across from him met his gaze for a second, then quickly looked away. He tried to look down and concentrate on finding the novel, but he found he couldn't wrench his gaze away from her face. She sighed again and looked at him, holding his gaze for a fraction longer this time. When she looked away the second time, Luke began to wonder what was wrong with him. He tried several times to look away, but he couldn't do it for more than a few seconds. Not wanting her to turn her disapproving gaze on him for a third time, he abandoned his search and settled back in his seat, closing his eyes. But not completely. Through tiny slits, he continued to watch the girl as she pointedly stared out of the window.

She was beautiful. Perhaps not in a conventional sense; she certainly wasn't dressed to impress. But it wasn't her appearance that had him hooked. There was something about her that drew him in, almost forcing him to look at her. He shifted about in his seat, trying to get comfortable in his fake sleeping position. He saw the girl flick a glance at him, then look down at her bag, then look around the crowded train. Luke's heart constricted as he realised that she seemed to be deciding whether to stay sitting there or to find somewhere else. Bizarrely, considering he didn't know her name and had never heard her voice, Luke knew he couldn't bear for her to get up and leave now. What if he never saw her again?

He took in a deep, slow breath, opened his eyes and forced himself to stare out of the window. It helped that the reflection of the window meant that he could still see her. Tiny changes in her facial expression gave Luke the impression that she was having a pretty intense internal monologue. He wondered what she was thinking and why she had looked at him the way she had. Maybe she was just sick of strange men chatting her up and was trying to deter him. Or maybe she felt attracted to him but had a boyfriend, or even a husband.

Luke's gaze flicked down to her left hand. No ring, but that didn't mean she was definitely single. He moved his gaze back to her reflection, only lingering for a moment on her tanned, smooth, bare leg.

The girl frowned, closed her eyes and shook her head, causing Luke to wonder again what she was thinking. He tried to come up with an interesting opening to a conversation. Something that wouldn't make her feel awkward or send her running away screaming, or worse still - make her fall asleep. He'd never been very good at chatting up girls; he was normally far too shy. In his very few past relationships, the girls had usually chatted him up. Of course, once they got to know him and he'd relaxed, it was difficult to shut him up, especially when he got onto his favourite subjects. Luke yawned suddenly and blinked. *Come on,* he told himself. *Focus on the matter at hand, what do I say to her?*

He saw her hand clutch at her bag a little tighter and she glanced at her watch. Luke knew that if he didn't say something in the next thirty seconds, she might move on. Gathering all the courage he had, he swallowed hard and then spoke.

"So have you been to Barcelona before?"

His voice sounded weird to his own ears, and his stupid question echoed all around him as people glanced at him to see who he was speaking to. He watched the girl openly now, hoping that she would answer and not make him feel any more ridiculous than he already felt. She looked at him, her gaze piercing. He noticed now that she had bright blue eyes, with tiny flecks of grey running through them.

In a controlled, almost hostile voice, she answered. "Yes, thank you."

Luke blinked, confused by her tone. Her accent was too subtle to pick out where she was from. She could have been English, but then she could have been American or Canadian, too.

"Do you like it there? I've never been there before." Grimacing internally at his banal questions, Luke waited for her response, hoping for more this time.

She appeared to be struggling with something when she replied. "It's okay. I prefer Paris."

Definitely American, probably East Coast, Luke decided. Maybe she was just being hostile because she was American; he'd heard that they could be quite rude to people when they were travelling.

"Why aren't you in Paris then?" he joked, badly.

He saw her mutter something under her breath. He wasn't sure, but it looked like 'I wish I was'. Luke frowned. American or not, there really was no need for her rudeness. He considered shutting up and actually going to sleep. But something compelled him to ignore his wounded ego - and the humiliation of the other passengers watching him completely bomb - and continue.

"I've never been to Paris, maybe I'll go there on my next holiday. I only chose Barcelona because the deal was cheap and it was leaving at the right time. Though, after all the problems I've had getting here, it's not turned out to be very cheap, after all."

The girl nodded without commenting. Luke thought she looked like she was wondering why the hell he was still trying to talk to her. Why was he? It made no sense, not even to himself. He'd never felt like this before. He wondered idly if he was being possessed by something.

"Make sure you go in the spring, to Paris. It's beautiful then."

Luke smiled at the lady with the Australian accent sat next to him, hoping that she wouldn't take it as an invitation to keep talking.

"My husband took me there for our tenth anniversary in April and it was wonderful. Wasn't too hot either, at that time of year. Just the right temperature I think, no need for heavy clothes, but you don't melt either. We were going to go up the Eiffel Tower, but my husband is afraid of heights and I didn't want to go up by myself, what would be the point in that? Maybe I'll go back one day with..."

Luke turned from the Australian lady, trying to tune her out. The girl looked like she was trying not to smile; she even looked a little bit smug that she'd been let off the hook by the kind lady who wouldn't shut up. She was now going on about the French bread and how they'd had a perfect picnic in the park by the Louvre.

How could he try and strike up a conversation with the girl now? Luke wished he'd been raised to be a little less polite, then he would have told the Australian to shut up while he tried to talk to the girl. However, he was doing such a terrible job of it, maybe she was just saving him the further embarrassment of being snubbed again.

Another passenger across the carriage decided to join in the conversation, asking a question about Paris, so the Australian lady moved to a seat closer to her. Soon they were chatting away, ignoring Luke completely. Luke was relieved. He only had an hour and a half left of his journey to try and connect with the girl. First things first, he really wanted to know her name.

He decided to go for the direct approach.

"My name's Luke."

The girl raised an eyebrow, as if to say 'lucky you', but said nothing.

Luke wanted to kick something in frustration. Why was she being so aloof? Would it really kill her to be polite and reciprocate?

"Are you on holiday? Whereabouts in America are you from?" There. She couldn't possibly avoid direct questions like that without being unbelievably rude. Though so far, it didn't seem like she cared what other people thought of her.

"No, I'm not on holiday. And no, I'm not American, either."

Luke waited for her to elaborate, but apparently she wasn't going to. Just then, an announcement cut through the tense silence, naming the next station stop. With the slightest nod of her head to Luke, the girl all but jumped out of her seat and left the carriage as soon as the train rolled to a stop. Luke watched her slim form race down the platform to the exit. He swore under his breath.

After a few moments of indecision, he leapt up, ignored the looks he received from the other passengers, and stepped through the doors a second before they closed. Now what? He had no choice but to run. He slung the rucksack on his back, suddenly glad that his suitcase had been lost, because he would never have been able to pursue the girl if he'd had it with him.

His feet flew down the platform and he made his way out of the station, doing his best not to flatten anyone in the process. He stopped for a second outside and scanned the street in front of him. A flurry of movement at the end of the street caught his attention and before he'd fully processed it, he was off again. His rucksack thumped against his back, making his shirt stick to the sweat running down it. The Spanish sun that he'd been looking forward to now just seemed cruel.

He reached the end of the street and turned the corner. He skidded to a stop and stepped back. The girl was just a few metres away, leaning into the open window of a taxi. She glanced around her, then opened the passenger door and jumped in.

The taxi sped off, giving Luke only seconds to leap out into the road, frantically trying to flag a taxi, or in fact, anyone, down. He couldn't lose her now. Moments later, another taxi came into sight and Luke threw himself into the back of it, shouting for the taxi driver to follow the taxi in front.

Luckily, the driver must have been a film fan and understood him, because he put his foot down and within a minute, they were just a couple of cars behind. Luke gripped onto the headrest of the front passenger seat, his eyes glued on the taxi in front. His heart was thumping, and he briefly wondered why he was acting like an insane man, but then decided that it didn't matter. He felt more alive chasing after this girl than he had felt in his entire life. Screw logical and sensible - what he was doing was utterly crazy, but it felt completely right.

He barely noticed the buildings they passed as the taxi sped down the sometimes scarily narrow streets. At least the driver seemed to be having a good time. Luke's insane actions had brightened up at least one person's day.

- 189 -

The taxi came to a stop suddenly and Luke saw the girl get out of the taxi up ahead.

"How much?" he asked the driver frantically, scrabbling for his wallet in his back pocket. Without waiting to hear the reply, Luke pulled out a wad of euros and threw them onto the front seat. He jumped out of the taxi and hurried up the narrow path, trying to keep the girl in his sights. He lost her briefly as she turned a corner, so he started to jog. When he reached the corner, however, he slowed to a walk, which was good, because otherwise he would have ploughed into her and knocked her over.

She glared at him with unabashed annoyance as he fought to slow his heartbeat down.

"Are you following me?"

He opened his mouth to explain, but found that there really was no acceptable explanation. After floundering for a few moments, he said the only thing he could think of.

"I'm sorry."

She raised her eyebrows and then sighed. "Wasn't I clear enough on the train? I don't want to speak to you."

Luke frowned. "Why not?"

She shrugged. "I just don't, okay? Now please leave me alone." She turned to leave but Luke reached out and grabbed her.

When his hand touched her bare arm, the familiarity of her soft skin made his fingers tingle. Shocked, he held on tightly, not wanting to let her leave. She looked down at his hand, and again, a million unspoken thoughts and emotions played across her face.

"What do you want from me?" she whispered.

Luke shook his head. "I don't know. I'm sorry, I'm not normally this crazy, I promise. I just felt like I *needed* to speak to you. Please tell me your name."

The girl smiled, but it didn't reach her eyes. "Please just let me go. It's for the best, trust me."

Luke shook his head again, refusing to loosen his grip on her arm. "Just tell me your name, please."

The girl met his eyes and smiled her half smile again. "I will tell you my name if you let me go and promise not to follow me any further."

Luke nodded quickly and reluctantly let go of her arm, regretting the red mark that he left behind.

"My name is Ellie. Goodbye, Luke." With that, she ran down the street, disappearing into a building, leaving Luke staring after her, a feeling of sorrow lodged in his chest where his heart used to be.

$*$     $*$     $*$

Not again.

How had it happened? Ellie thought she'd done everything possible to avoid him, yet somehow he had managed to find her again. It was just crazy. What were the chances of him being on the same train, at the same time, in Spain, of all places? Maybe she should have just erred on the side of caution and stayed away from trains for the entire year. Then she'd probably have ended up meeting him on a plane or something. And to think she'd purposely moved to another country to avoid this situation happening again.

She leaned against the wooden door-frame and groaned. Perhaps she should have just hibernated for the year, then there would have been no chance of their paths crossing, would there?

Shaking her head at herself, she moved slowly down the hallway to the lounge, dumping her satchel on the sofa.

Her cat, Mañana, came to greet her; hungry, no doubt. Ellie went into the kitchen and began her normal evening routine. Feed the cat, make dinner, sit on the terrace and enjoy the sunshine. Okay, so moving to Spain definitely had its benefits. Ellie wished she had done it before, even if it hadn't really helped her when it came to Luke. Perhaps she should have moved to an island in the middle of the Pacific. Knowing her luck though, he would have found her there, too.

Her internal musings were interrupted by the peal of the doorbell. She froze in place and closed her eyes. *Please go away. Please.*

The doorbell went again. Her unspoken pleas turned into muttered expletives.

She gave it a few more minutes, but when it rang a third time, she knew that he wasn't going to give up. She looked around the lounge and wished it was a bit messier; it would have helped.

She walked as slowly as possible to the front door, dragging her bare feet across the cool tiles. She turned the key and pulled the door open slightly. She looked out and saw Luke's back as he paced up and down the path. He spun around at the sound of the creaking hinges.

"Look, before you say anything, I know I said I would leave you alone, but the truth is: I can't. I wish I knew why I'm acting like this, but I don't. I don't want to scare you, or annoy you; I just really want to talk to you, Ellie."

Ellie sighed. She opened the door a little wider and her shoulders slumped in defeat. "You'd better come in then."

Luke's eyes widened and she saw that she'd surprised him. He was probably expecting more resistance. Damn. Maybe she could have pushed him away if she'd tried a little harder. Too late now.

She stepped aside and waved him in, noticing with amusement how he almost ran up the steps. She closed the door and followed him into the lounge. Luke was stood in the middle, hands in his pockets, looking awkward.

"Would you like something to drink?"

He smiled at her. "Yes, please." He pulled the rucksack off his back and placed it on the settee.

Ellie went into the kitchen to make the drinks, gesturing for him to follow her. Out on the terrace, they settled onto the loungers and she silently sipped her drink while she tried to figure out what to say to him. She'd never been at a loss for words around him before, but this time was different. This time, she wanted to change things, but her plans were already in ruins. She needed a new plan, and fast.

"Thank you for not calling the police. Following you like that was, well, the weirdest thing I've ever done, and I'm sorry if I scared you. I just wanted, well, actually, I just *needed* to talk to you."

Ellie sat up a little and smiled at him. "Don't worry, you didn't scare me, Luke. I don't scare that easily."

Luke smiled back, relief radiating from him. He sat up as well, leaning toward Ellie as he spoke again.

"You're being rather calm about a complete stranger following you to your home, then getting himself invited in for a drink. Is this a regular thing for you?"

Ellie laughed then, the sound echoed off the low white walls of the terrace. She shook her head. "No, this isn't a regular thing. It's complicated to explain why I feel safe with you, Luke."

Luke frowned. "Please try to explain."

Ellie sighed, her smile slipping away. "It's never been like this before. I've never explained it before. I've just, well, pretended. But I'm tired of pretending, it never changes anything in the end. It doesn't matter what I do, or how I do it or when I do it," Ellie jumped up, her agitation causing her to pace the tiny terrace. "I don't understand. This time, I was sure that if I changed us, that if we didn't meet, it would be enough to change everything. But here you are again!" She flung her arm out at him, almost accusingly. "And here we go, again. It's never going to end, is it?"

She stopped her frantic pacing and stared down at him, her hands on her hips.

Luke looked up at her in confusion. "I have absolutely no idea what you're on about. But it sounds like," he stood up and took a hesitant step toward her, "we've met before?"

Ellie sighed. "Yes. More than once."

Luke reached for her, and as his hand touched her bare skin again, the electric current between them was undeniable.

"That would explain why I feel so drawn to you," Luke

murmured. "But if we've met before, how come I don't remember?"

Ellie closed the gap between them and laid her head on his chest. She felt him wrap his arms around her and rest his chin on the top of her head. How could she possibly have avoided this? Why would she want to, when it felt so good?

"I don't know where to start," she whispered.

Luke tightened his hold on her. "The beginning is always a good place."

Ellie chuckled. "That's the problem, there is no beginning. There is no end either; it's just one continuous loop."

There was silence then, punctuated only by a bird in a nearby tree and the sounds of cars passing the front of the house.

"Perhaps we should have another drink first. I get the feeling that this is going to be a very long and complicated explanation."

Ellie laughed again and pulled back a little. "I'll get the drinks. Would you like a shower, too?"

Luke raised an eyebrow. "Do I smell that bad?"

Ellie bit her lip. "Um, no, I just thought, you know, sometimes it's nice to freshen up after travelling."

Luke smiled at her blatant lie. "Okay, that would be good, actually. Though I'm afraid the airline lost my luggage, so I don't have any spare clothes."

"Not a problem. I have some clothes upstairs that an old room-mate left behind. They should fit you."

"In that case, lead the way."

*The Elphite is available in paperback and on Kindle from Amazon.*

# Earth Angel Sanctuary

A safe space to Learn, Grow, Heal and Evolve.

The Earth Angel Sanctuary is an online space where Earth Angels can watch videos on the 'basics' to shifting emotions with advanced energy clearings, rituals, interviews plus so much more, all to help Earth Angels help themselves.

Founded by Sarah Rebecca Vine in 2014, the Earth Angel Sanctuary has several contributors and has new videos and information added to it every month.

To join simply visit:

## earthangelsanctuary.com

You can sign up for a monthly or yearly membership.

*In gratitude for the nourishing vibrational energy of the trees that have sustained me for so many years, I have created:*

# Sacred Tree Spirit

In this dream-like space, you can receive vibrational therapies and core-belief re-programming to improve emotional and physical health.
You can relax in the healing crystal spa, watch life-affirming films in the imaginarium, attend courses and purchase unique handmade gifts in the backcountry homestore.

I look forward to connecting with you!

sacred-tree-spirit.com

designs from a
different planet

madappledesigns
.co.uk

# Peace of Stone

*Harmony for Heart & Home*

## In our Shop

Gifts ● Crystals ● Jewellery ● Incense
● Essential Oils ● Angels ● Books

Like us on ⬛ or follow Peace of Stone on ⬛
keep updated on upcoming events and exclusive offers

Tel: 01600 714303 E-mail: peaceofstone@hotmail.co.uk

## www.peaceofstone.com

# Zenith

Crystals♥Jewellery♥Books
Ethical & Fair Trade Gifts
Readings♥Talks♥Workshops

16a Corn Square, Leominster, Hereford,
Herefordshire

01568 613145

Mon - Fri: 10:00–17:00
Sat: 10:00–16:00

# This book was published by The Amethyst Angel.

A selection of books bought to publication by The Amethyst Angel. To view more of our published books visit **theamethystangel.com**

We have a selection of publishing packages available or we can tailor a package to suit each author's individual needs and budget. We also run workshops for groups and individuals on 'How to publish' your own books.

For more information on Independent publishing packages and workshops offered by The Amethyst Angel, please visit **theamethystangel.com**

Manufactured by Amazon.ca
Bolton, ON